Michael Bar-Zohar

KU-447-604

The Spy who Died Twice

Translated from the French by
June P Wilson and Walter B Michaels

Futura Publications Limited
A Contact Book

A Contact Book

First published in Great Britain in 1975
by Weidenfeld and Nicolson

First Futura Publications edition 1976
published in association with Weidenfeld
and Nicolson

ISBN 0 8600 7400 5
Printed in Great Britain by
Richard Clay (The Chaucer Press) Ltd,
Bungay, Suffolk

Futura Publications Limited
110 Warner Road, London SE5

For Ines

Prologue

GIRLS WERE SHRIEKING.

One of them was writing on the ground near a clay mound studded with hundreds of candles that flickered in the wind. Feet thrashing, her head shaking back and forth, she let out a stream of piercing screams. A whitish foam covered her half-open mouth as her body rolled between the ritual designs chalked on the black earth. Above her stood a crude wooden cross crowned with an old bowler hat and wrapped in a black frock coat, its coattails flapping like some monstrous bird. It was the symbol of horror: Baron Samedi, the god of death.

The emaciated sorcerer, eyes shut, swayed to the rhythm of the tom-toms. Slowly, he pulled a long machete from his belt and raised it high above his head. The gleaming blade reflected the baleful red glow of the coals. The tom-toms' rhythm quickened. The shrieks of the girls merged into one long inhuman cry.

Suddenly, the old black man crouched over his victim. Eyes opened wide, lips and nostrils quivering, his breath coming in spasms, he let out a single rasping scream. With a savage swing, he brandished the knife — and struck.

Blood spurted from the severed neck. It splashed on the sorcerer's shirt and formed a dark puddle at the feet of Baron Samedi's altar.

With trembling hands, the old man brought a gourd to his lips, took a large gulp and spat out a spray of liquid over the girls dancing frenetically around him. The strong smell of rum wafted through the night air.

Now the staccato beat of the tom-toms drowned out the cries. A sudden burst of flame from the base of the altar bathed the drummer's face in an orange color.

Baron Samedi, the most terrible of the voodoo gods, had taken his victim.

Across the folder's cover was inscribed in purple ink:

CURRENT FILE 426/11
Document No. 1 out of a total of 8 documents
Classification: Nonclassified

ASSOCIATED PRESS, PORT-AU-PRINCE, HAITI, 10/19 18:45.   AN
UNIDENTIFIED BODY WAS DISCOVERED YESTERDAY NEAR THE
SUBURB OF PETIONVILLE BY THE HAITIAN POLICE.   THE POLICE
ARE CONSIDERING THE POSSIBILITY THAT IT MAY BE THE VIC-
TIM OF A RITUAL VOODOO SACRIFICE.   THE BODY WAS ALMOST
COMPLETELY INCINERATED AND WAS FOUND BURIED AT THE
SUMMIT OF A HILL WHICH SERVES AS SANCTUARY FOR A FANAT-
ICAL SECT OF VOODOO PRACTITIONERS.   THE CORPSE APPEARS
TO BE THAT OF A WHITE MALE.   MORE TO COME . . .

Document No. 2 out of a total of 8 documents
Classification: Nonclassified

ASSOCIATED PRESS, PORT-AU-PRINCE, HAITI, 10/19 21:00. EIGHTEEN HAITIANS, ELEVEN MEN AND SEVEN WOMEN, HAVE BEEN ARRESTED BY THE POLICE AT PORT-AU-PRINCE AND ARE BEING INTERROGATED CONCERNING THE MYSTERIOUS DEATH OF AN UNIDENTIFIED WHITE MAN WHOSE BODY WAS DISCOVERED YESTERDAY ON THE COLLINE DES ESPRITS NEAR PETIONVILLE. THE SUSPECTS BELONG TO A SECT OF VOODOO FANATICS WHO PERFORM ANIMAL SACRIFICES DURING THEIR RITUAL CEREMONIES EVERY SATURDAY. THE "HOUGAN" AND THE "MAMBO," THE SECT'S PRIEST AND PRIESTESS, 60 AND 57 YEARS OLD RESPECTIVELY, HAVE BEEN PREACHING FOR YEARS THE REVIVAL OF HUMAN SACRIFICE AS IT WAS PRACTICED DURING THE REIGN OF KING CHRISTOPHE. THE SECT MEETS REGULARLY IN SECRET, AND THE REGION'S INHABITANTS TAKE CARE TO AVOID THE COLLINE DES ESPRITS ON SATURDAY NIGHTS FOR FEAR OF THEIR LIVES. OFFICIAL SOURCES SAY THE POLICE FOUND FRESH BLOOD STAINS AT THE FOOT OF BARON SAMEDI'S ALTAR, VERY NEAR THE SPOT WHERE THE BODY WAS BURIED. IT HAS NOT YET BEEN ESTABLISHED IF THE BODY WAS BURNED DURING THE COURSE OF THE CEREMONY, OR AFTER IN ORDER TO MAKE IDENTIFICATION IMPOSSIBLE. THE SPOKESMAN FOR THE PORT-AU-PRINCE POLICE HAS CATEGORICALLY REFUSED TO REVEAL HOW THE POLICE WERE INFORMED OF THE MURDER AND THE LOCATION OF THE BURIAL. SINCE THE BODY WAS THAT OF A WHITE MAN, THE POLICE ARE CONDUCTING INVESTIGATIONS AMONG THE WHITE POPULATION OF PORT-AU-PRINCE AND IN THE HOTELS, TO LEARN IF ANYONE DISAPPEARED SATURDAY, OCTOBER 14, THE PRESUMED DATE OF THE MURDER. THE SPOKESMAN ADDED THAT THE PERSONS DETAINED HAVE DENIED ANY CONNECTION WITH THE MURDER. MORE TO COME . . .

Document No. 3 out of a total of 8 documents
Classification:　Nonclassified

ASSOCIATED PRESS, PORT-AU-PRINCE, HAITI 10/19 23:55. THE
POLICE ARE CONDUCTING AN EXHAUSTIVE SEARCH IN PORT-AU-
PRINCE, PETIONVILLE, KENSCOFF AND CAP-HAITIEN FOR AN ENG-
LISH TOURIST, AGED 60, WHO DISAPPEARED FROM HIS HOTEL
IN PETIONVILLE, SATURDAY 10/14, A FEW HOURS BEFORE THE
DEATH OF THE WHITE MAN ASSASSINATED DURING THE COURSE
OF A BARBAROUS VOODOO CEREMONY ON THE COLLINE DES ES-
PRITS. THE TOURIST WAS A WELL-KNOWN ANTHROPOLOGIST
WHO SPECIALIZED IN ANCIENT RELIGIONS AND PRIMITIVE RITES.
HE WAS KNOWN TO HAVE A PARTICULAR INTEREST IN VOODOO.
IN CONVERSATIONS WITH HOTEL GUESTS HE HAD OFTEN EX-
PRESSED A DESIRE TO WATCH AN AUTHENTIC VOODOO CERE-
MONY, RATHER THAN WHAT HE TERMED "THE TOURIST SPEC-
TACULARS" PRESENTED SEVERAL TIMES A WEEK AT
L'HABITATION LECLERC IN PORT-AU-PRINCE. THE HAITIAN PO-
LICE REFUSE TO REVEAL HIS IDENTITY UNTIL THE INVESTIGA-
TION IS CONCLUDED. THE EIGHTEEN MEMBERS OF A FANATIC
VOODOO SECT, ARRESTED EARLY IN THE AFTERNOON, CONTINUE
TO PROTEST THAT THEY HAD NO CONNECTION WHATEVER WITH
THE MURDER. THEY CLAIM THAT ONLY A SMALL WHITE GOAT
WAS SACRIFICED DURING THE CEREMONY ON SATURDAY 10/14.

Document No. 4 out of a total of 8 documents
Classification: Nonclassified

ASSOCIATED PRESS, PORT-AU-PRINCE, HAITI, 10/20 08:17.   IN
AN OFFICIAL COMMUNIQUE, THE POLICE IN PORT-AU-PRINCE
REVEALED THIS MORNING THAT THE INCINERATED BODY FOUND
10/18 ON THE COLLINE DES ESPRITS AT PETIONVILLE IS NOT,
REPEAT NOT, THAT OF THE ENGLISH ANTHROPOLOGIST, AGED
60, WHOSE DISAPPEARANCE WAS DISCLOSED LAST NIGHT.   THE
MISSING TOURIST HAS STILL NOT BEEN FOUND, BUT AN
ANTHROPOMETRIC EXAMINATION OF THE CORPSE HAS ES-
TABLISHED BEYOND A DOUBT THAT IT IS NOT THAT OF THE
ENGLISHMAN IN QUESTION.   THE MAN WHO DISAPPEARED IS
SMALL, NOT OVER FIVE FOOT FOUR, WHEREAS THE CORPSE AP-
PEARS TO BE THAT OF A MAN OVER SIX FEET TALL.

Document No. 5 out of a total of 8 documents
Classification: Nonclassified

ASSOCIATED PRESS, PORT-AU-PRINCE, HAITI, 10/24 16:35.   THE
INVESTIGATION OF THE BRUTAL MURDER OF A WHITE MAN
DURING THE COURSE OF A VOODOO CEREMONY IN HAITI AP-
PEARS TO HAVE REACHED AN IMPASSE. CAPTAIN JULIEN LE-
FEVRE OF THE CRIMINAL DIVISION ADMITTED BEFORE A GROUP
OF JOURNALISTS THAT ATTEMPTS TO IDENTIFY THE VICTIM AND
HIS KILLERS HAVE BEEN FRUITLESS.   HE ALSO INDICATED THAT
SOME AND PERHAPS ALL THE SUSPECTS ARRESTED AFTER THE
DISCOVERY OF THE MURDER MAY BE RELEASED ON BAIL.

Document No. 6 out of a total of 8 documents
Classification: TOP-SECRET
435/7/723

Sent from: Port-au-Prince, 10/25
Received at: Washington, 10/26
Decoded by: 427/3/21
Origin: Cassandra
Destination: Sheba
Attention of:

> Central Intelligence Agency (C.I.A.)
> Director for Latin America
> Latin America / Department Chief, Haiti
> C.I.A. Central Archives
> Liaison Officer F.B.I.

Subject: Ritual murder in Haiti

1. I would like to call to your attention a certain number
of unusual facts concerning the murder of a white man on
the Colline des Esprits in Pétionville, near Port-au-Prince,
Haiti, on October 14. (See press dispatches 10/19, 10/20,
10/24.)

2. In my previous reports, I gave you the code number
for the resident M.I.6 * agent in Haiti. He lives at 117 Rue
du Roi Christophe, in Port-au-Prince, and uses as his cover
the identity of the Reverend Thomas Finchley, an Anglican
priest who distributes funds to provide aid and education
for needy children. His cover may be authentic. In any
event, it allows Father Finchley to move about the island
freely without raising suspicion. Finchley is also known
for his strenuous opposition to ritual voodoo ceremonies.

---

* M.I.6: The British Secret Service operating abroad. It was recently re-
named the S.I.S. — Secret Intelligence Service.

3. On 10/16 at 5:30 A.M., a black Haitian knocked on Father Finchley's door and awakened his maid, Josephine Bernadette, a woman of sixty-five. The stranger, a man of about thirty, was simply dressed and spoke to her in the local dialect. He said to her: "Wake up your master right away. Tell him we've prepared a *cabri sans cornes* for him and that it's buried five paces to the right of Baron Samedi on the Colline des Esprits. Tell your master, but no one else."

4. The stranger turned on his heels, leaving the old woman flabbergasted. She hadn't even had time to tell him that her master had left during the evening, that he'd been summoned to Bounou, a distant village in the region of the Étang Saumâtre, where a typhus epidemic had broken out. Therefore it would seem that the mysterious stranger had no knowledge of Finchley's absence. I should add that when the messenger arrived, the old servant was already in a very agitated state. That same evening, before his departure, Finchley had received several telephone calls. The caller had hung up each time Finchley picked up the telephone.

5. Josephine Bernadette was terrified when she heard the message. *Cabri sans cornes* is the voodoo name for human sacrifice. Human sacrifices used to be frequent, but the authorities insist that they have ceased altogether for at least a century. Nevertheless, the mere mention of the name is enough to strike terror in superstitious Haitians. And regardless of what the authorities say, the public believes that human sacrifices are still being practiced, although rarely and in secret. Those still practicing the ritual are thought to be the "Hougans" of the Red Sect who go by the name of "Vin 'Bain Ding" (Blood, Pain, Excrement). The ritual murder is based on the belief that every life must be paid for by another. Thus, a man who desires the death of his enemy must offer a human sacrifice to Baron Samedi.

Usually in this type of ceremony it is babies who are sacrificed. However, occasionally adults are killed, and the body
incinerated afterward.

6. Josephine Bernadette kept her secret for two days,
awaiting her master's return. But when he failed to come
back, the old woman grew too fearful to sleep. She is a fer-
vent Catholic, but it's said of the Haitians that if 90 percent
believe in Christ 100 percent believe in voodoo. Baron Samedi is the most cruel of all the voodoo divinities: he is the
"loa" of the spirits and of the dead. On 10/18, Josephine
Bernadette could no longer keep her secret and divulged it
to Emilie Lafourquet — the "Mambo" or chief voodoo
priestess in Haiti. The priestess ordered her to remain silent, but she herself alerted the police, probably out of fear
of the authorities.

7. Several detectives from the Port-au-Prince police force
immediately went to the Colline des Esprits. It is a sinister
place which the inhabitants of Pétionville consider accursed.
They are convinced that the hill is haunted by the devil and
that "zombies" (the living dead) wander about by night.
Baron Samedi's altar is on the summit of the hill, and con-
sists of a wooden cross crowned with a bowler hat and
draped in a black frock coat. Every Saturday, the members
of a small fanatic sect gather there and sacrifice a young goat
or chicken to the Baron.

8. The body was found in the exact place indicated by the
mysterious stranger — five paces to the right of the altar. It
was buried two feet deep. The body was completely incinerated except for the right hand. The cause of the death
could not be precisely determined, although the corpse bore
several knife wounds. The man was dead before they
burned his body.

9. The dead man has still not been identified. At first the

police thought the victim was an English anthropologist named David Jennings, 60, who was in Haiti doing research. Jennings had left his hotel, the Villa Antillaise in Pétionville, on Saturday the 14th, the presumed day of the murder. He is still on the books as having disappeared. But an examination of the body proved conclusively that the dead man is not Jennings.

10. The police have not yet been able to determine if the blood in front of the altar is that of the dead man or some animal offered in sacrifice. The Haitian police do not possess the equipment necessary to make this kind of examination.

11. My conclusions:

a) The victim is a white man, either resident or tourist.

b) The killers probably knew the Reverend Finchley's identity, and that he belonged to the British Secret Service. If they tried to warn him, it was undoubtedly to make sure he would be the first to learn of the assassination and to examine the body.

c) The fact that the body was completely incinerated except for the right hand is no doubt revealing. The assassins probably wanted to facilitate Finchley's identification of the body by its fingerprints.

d) The assassins were careful not to alert the police in Port-au-Prince about the murder.

e) The victim was no doubt involved in Finchley's secret activities. He might have been a British agent or, on the other hand, an enemy agent. The discovery of the body and the uncovering of the affair are obviously due to pure chance. If Finchley had been home to receive the message — as the assassins supposed — he would have been the only one to know anything. The anonymous telephone calls to Finchley the night of the murder were surely from the assassins, who wanted to make certain that he was at home. He was called away into the interior only a short time after the last call.

12) I suggest that appropriate services in the Intelligence Community * start an investigation to determine the identity of the dead man from an examination of his fingerprints (see attached).

13) The fingerprints of the right hand are as follows:

| V 2672 | V 41213 | V 32712 | V 3385 | V 32539 |
| V 7174 | V 4285 | V 7268 | V 4726 | V 4299 |

14) Attached pages: Enlargements of the fingerprints.

* Intelligence Community: Term describing the sum total of American agencies and services specializing in espionage, counterespionage, secret activities and special operations: the C.I.A., F.B.I., National Security Agency, Secret Services, Defense Intelligence Agency, etc.

Document No. 7 out of a total of 8 documents
Classification: TOP-SECRET

Department of Justice
F.B.I.
Central Archives
7456/76/485

10/30 Washington, D.C.
Destination: Central Intelligence Agency — Director for
Latin-America/ Department Chief, Haiti/
Archives
Intermediary: Liaison Officer, F.B.I.
Subject: Copy of your 435/7/723 of 10/25–10/26
1. Results of the examination of fingerprints attached to
your letter 435/7/723 at the Central Archives are negative.
2. Examinations have also been made by the following
departments: Foreign/A and Foreign/B; F.B.I.; Drugs and
Narcotics; Secret Service (President and V.I.P.). All results
also negative.

Steven Kranz
Director, Central Archives

Document No. 8 out of a total of 8 documents
Classification: TOP-SECRET

Central Intelligence Agency
Central Archives/ Dept. of Foreign Services/ Great Britain
M.I.6

1/11 Washington, D.C.
482/75/63/2
Destination: Director for Latin-America/ Department
              Chief, Haiti

Information Copy: Director C.I.A.
Subject: Cassandra Report 435/7/723 of 10/25–10/26
1) The fingerprints attached to Cassandra Report
435/7/723 are identical to those fingerprints on the attached
sheet.

> Roger Ackerman, Jr., Director
> Department of Central Archives

The young man compared the photographs for several moments. The fingerprints were identical. He turned the sheet over. The photograph on the back was that of a thin-faced man with pale cold eyes and drawn lips. His chin was a bit lantern-jawed; his blond hair was parted on the left side.

"It isn't possible," he said, looking at the familiar face once again. And at the name written below.

"You recognize him, Jeff?" asked Jim Sullivan, the C.I.A. director.

He nodded.

"You remember?" Sullivan went on.

"I sure do," Jeff Saunders replied. With slow mechanical motions, he put the documents back in the folder, placed the identity sheet on top and pushed the pile toward his boss.

"That man has been dead for over a year," he said. "I was there when he was buried. I even left some flowers on his grave. Chrysanthemums, I think."

Part One

A Year Ago in Saint-Tropez

1

A YEAR AGO . . .

On that spring evening — it was May 16th — clouds of smoke enveloped Saint-Tropez, the most publicized resort in Europe. Rhythmic salvos reverberated through the narrow streets and on the jetty of the old fishing port. The acrid smell of gunpowder hung in the air which vibrated to the sound of fife and drums. Groups of soldiers dressed in Napoleonic costumes with cocked hats, white trousers and blue coats piped in red moved slowly through the picturesque streets. From time to time, the men stopped, broke ranks and stood in a circle around the effigy of a mustached saint decked out with crown and medals which was borne aloft by four vigorous young men. A heavy-set captain would join the circle, brandishing a pike which he shook at the four points of the compass while solemnly bowing to the crowd assembled around him. At his orders, the soldiers aimed their sawed-off muskets at the foot of the effigy and fired off a series of deafening salvos.

These trigger-happy grenadiers-for-a-day were actually Saint-Tropez shopkeepers, waiters, postmen and fishermen.

Once a year, they dressed up in the colorful uniforms of the Imperial Army, borrowed the muskets from the basement of the municipal museum and invaded the streets and squares of their town to celebrate the *bravade* of Saint-Tropez. Thus did they pay homage to their ancestors' bravery, which had repelled many a foreign attack on their port long before Brigitte Bardot ever thought to peel off her clothes on the peninsula's golden sands. Wreathed in smoke and heralded by bellicose whistles, drum rolls and bugle blasts, the grenadiers burst into the imposing Quai Suffren which faced the sea. Hordes of children, their eyes bright with excitement, galloped at their heels. The *bravadeurs* moved toward the center of the square under the bored gaze of movie producers and Italian playboys lying on the decks of the sleek yachts moored in the port. The Midi's celebrated chefs appeared on the stoops of their restaurants as the Provençal smells of garlic, fennel, thyme, frogs' legs and bouillabaisse drifted around them. Exquisitely bronzed starlets and models in transparent shirts stretched in the deep chairs of the Café Sénéquier to catch a glimpse of the lusty warriors. Scandinavian nymphets, French girl-chasers, American hippies and even a pair of blond Lesbians escorted by a greyhound, pressed against the police cordon. The deafening noise of the salvos had reached such a pitch that the crowd was reluctantly forced into silence.

Suddenly, in the stillness between two bursts of gunfire, the sound of a woman's scream pierced the air.

The body lay on the rear deck of the yacht *Anna-Maria*, near the guardrail, a few feet from the polished gangplank leading to the jetty. The man was on his back, his arms spread wide. A white sailing cap with gold stripes had fallen on the deck near his handsome graying head. His wide-open blue eyes still reflected amazement. Shards from a broken glass of champagne were scattered near his right hand, and the pale yellow liquid had begun to merge with the blood oozing from his body. He was dressed in a navy blue blazer, tan trousers and white loafers. The blazer was riddled with ugly bloodstained holes. The elegant shirt of Swiss voile and the Cardin foulard around his neck were also torn and soaked with blood.

"What a mess!" Inspector Berrichon said, stepping distastefully around the body. He dropped into a chair next to the round table on which a champagne bottle stood in a silver wine cooler. The inspector grasped the bottle, raised it to eye level and gauged the contents with a distracted air. Then he looked around him.

"Only one glass," he said.

"Only one glass, sir," echoed Ciboulé, a policeman, in the melodious accent of Provence. He was shifting from one foot to the other, not knowing if he was supposed to stand at attention before the inspector. "The dead man's glass, sir. It looks as if he was the only one on deck when he was shot." And he added hastily, "And the only one on board. He had a big crew, about twenty, I think, but he'd given them the afternoon off and had stayed here alone."

"Alone? What about the English girl? Where is she?"

"She's below, in the saloon, sir. Lieutenant Sauvageot is interrogating her. She claims the man was already dead when she came aboard."

"Of course. Naturally," the inspector said sarcastically. "Tell Sauvageot I want to see him. And call in reinforcements. We may run into some trouble with this crowd."

He looked at the growing sea of people on the quay and muttered, "Jesus, he sure picked a great place to get bumped off! In the middle of a Saint-Tropez *bravade*. Look at that mob, for Christ's sake! . . ."

The Quai Suffren was literally boiling over. Thousands

of people were elbowing each other, lunging in waves against the phalanx of policemen hurriedly summoned to protect the yacht. The police kept trying to push them back toward the row of shops and cafés on the far side of the esplanade. The sensational news of the murder on the fabulous yacht had spread like brush fire. In the space of fifteen minutes, anybody on the Côte d'Azur who could walk seemed to have found his way to the yacht basin at Saint-Tropez. The *bravade* had broken up and the Napoleonic grenadiers had joined the crowd, dragging their antique guns, their fancy-dress uniforms rubbing shoulders with the latest creations of Courrèges and Pucci. It took the combined power of a dozen policemen's elbows, shoulders and fists to clear a way for the team of experts rushed in from Marseilles.

"They're going crazy back at headquarters," Dr. Leblanc, the coroner, reported to Inspector Berrichon. "The Minister of the Interior has already telephoned twice and the Greek Consul has cut short his holiday."

The crowd continued to press against the police barricade. "Is it really Theodoris?" cooed a charming creature in a shirt open to the waist of her rump-hugging pants.

"It's him all right," volunteered a professional Casanova as he edged his way with a hungry smile toward the owner of the décolletage.

"It's him all right," said Lieutenant Émile Sauvageot to Inspector Berrichon. "Manoli Theodoris. The biggest ship-owner in the world. And the richest man in Europe."

Inspector Berrichon sighed. Nothing like this had ever happened to him, at least not since his promotion to the rank of inspector and his appointment to Saint-Tropez. During the past two years he'd had only one murder and

that was almost by accident — some gangsters from Nice settling accounts after a holdup at the Crédit Lyonnais. One of
them had helped himself to an overlarge portion of the take;
his colleagues, feeling a bit injured, caught up with him in
the middle of the night in front of the Hôtel de Paris on the
outskirts of Saint-Tropez. The shoot-out left two dead and
one wounded, and the police were very gratified indeed.
Except for that incident, Inspector Berrichon had had little
more than a few drunken fights and the occasional sailor
who took liberties with the overexposed charms of the summer visitors. And, once in a while, the trumped-up suicide
of some cover girl, singer or movie star hungry for publicity.

It made this evening's incident all the more awkward: a
spectacular murder, virtually under the nose of thousands of
witnesses, on the deck of a sumptuous yacht. And to cap it
all, the victim was one of the richest men in the world —
Manoli Theodoris, king of oil and the seven seas. God only
knew what dark history lay behind this killing. Inspector
Berrichon was profoundly suspicious of these Greeks. Not
to mention this particular millionaire's shady deals and the
wild orgies — according to gossip — that took place on the
Anna-Maria.

"That's life," Sauvageot said with a laugh, as if he'd read
the inspector's thoughts. "One burst of shots and all his
millions aren't worth a sou."

"What burst of shots?" Berrichon said. "You think he was
killed with an automatic weapon?"

"Absolutely," Sauvageot replied. The commissioner was
young, with bright eyes and a mobile face that reflected considerable self-assurance. As usual, he had been among the
first to arrive on the scene and had already finished with his
preliminary investigation.

He took a small metal object from his pocket and placed it on the table next to the bottle of champagne.

"It's a nine-millimeter bullet. I got it out of the deck, over there." He pointed to one of the floorboards to the right of the body. Berrichon could just make out the hole and its slightly gouged edges. "There are a good many more bullets in the deck floor. The killers must have fired at least fifteen in a single volley. Eight of them hit Theodoris. The angle of fire, thirty to forty degrees from top to bottom. Theodoris was a big man — at least six feet. He was hit as he was leaning against the guardrail, holding his glass and watching the ceremony on the quay. Since I don't know of any eight-and-a-half-foot giants who could have got him from this angle, it seems clear that the shots must have come from a window in one of the houses on the other side of the esplanade."

"Well . . ." Berrichon didn't seem convinced and looked skeptically at the buildings across the way. For the most part they were old, sun-bleached four-story houses. Above one of the second-floor balconies, he could just make out "Hôtel Riviera" in tired gray letters.

"That's about a hundred and fifty feet," the inspector said. "It's practically impossible to hit a target at that range with an automatic weapon."

"Not if the weapon had a telescopic lens," Sauvageot said. "Several kinds of submachine guns take telescopic lenses. It makes firing child's play. Nine-millimeter is the standard caliber for several models. It's true that you can't put a silencer on it, but on a day like this you hardly need it. The man behind the gun took aim from one of those windows, then simply waited for the grenadiers' order to fire in the *bravade*. He fired at the same time they did. His gun certainly made less noise than the grenadiers' muskets."

"Damn well thought out, if you're right," Berrichon said. "The work of real professionals."

Sauvageot shook his head. "Professionals, maybe. But the execution was far from perfect. They had to work very fast. Eight out of fifteen bullets on target isn't all that great. Then look here: professionals don't leave souvenirs like this unless they're in a real hurry."

He handed the inspector two little golden cylinders. Berrichon inspected them with a look of surprise.

"Cartridge cases? Where the hell did you find these?"

"In the building on the left of the Hôtel Riviera. Third floor. Second window from the right."

Berrichon scowled as he tried to locate the window. It was hard to see because he was blinded by the floodlights set up on the roofs opposite to light the *bravade*.

"Yes, I see it," he said finally. "I think I see it. But there's someone up there. I think I see a head in the window."

"It's one of our men. The room is used for storage by a boutique on the ground floor called 'Popsy.' As soon as we got here, we figured out the angle of fire and calculated the trajectory. I immediately sent some men over to the house. They found the room right off — the door had been bashed in and there were cartridges all over the floor. The killers fired and lit out. We've set up roadblocks, and sea patrols are out, but I don't think we'll catch them. The weapon is probably already at the bottom of the sea, and we have no way of identifying the killer."

The inspector was examining the marks engraved on the bottom of the cartridge cases. "Made in Belgium," he said.

Sauvageot shrugged. "Half the bullets in the world are made in Belgium."

Berrichon let it pass. He glanced around the deck at the experts who were still at work, oblivious to the crowd watching their every move. Two young men were earnestly taking fingerprints, collecting bits of broken glass and removing bullets from the floor, making notes all the while. A photographer was leaping around the body, plying his flash with morbid delight. The coroner, his hands covered with blood, was making a methodical examination of the gaping wounds; he obviously felt quite at home digging around in 9-mm holes.

Berrichon turned to Sauvageot who was aimlessly lining up the cartridge cases around the wine cooler.

"What about the girl? Have you gotten anywhere with her?"

"She's down below," Sauvageot replied. "She's still in shock. I don't think she had anything to do with the murder."

The young detective took some sheets of paper from the pocket of his sweat-soaked shirt.

"Her name is . . . let's see . . . MacAlister, Sheila MacAlister. Twenty-eight. Unmarried. Address: 39 Warwick Road, Maida Vale, London W9. Employed by the British Admiralty — that's their navy department. She arrived at the Nice–Côte D'Azur Airport by direct flight from London — BEA Flight 467, at 16:25. She rented a Ford Taunus from Avis and arrived at Saint-Tropez at 19:15. She left the car in the port parking lot, five hundred yards from here, and came at a run. Two agents saw her dash the length of the jetty. They noticed her because the public had been forbidden access to the jetty on account of the *bravade*. They let her pass when she explained she was expected on the *Anna-Maria*. It was she who discovered the body and promptly went into hysterics. You could hear her scream hundreds of yards off."

"You arrested her?"

"What for?" Sauvageot looked at the inspector with surprise. "Her passport is valid and there's no reason to connect her with the crime. But to make certain, we could check with London."

Berrichon nodded agreement and wrote something down in his notebook. "What was she doing on the *Anna-Maria?*"

"She wouldn't tell me." Sauvageot smiled. "At first I thought she was Theodoris's companion for one of his famous cruises, although — frankly — I've seen them better looking. But take a look at what we found on her. She fought like a tiger to keep us from getting it."

Sauvageot handed the inspector a piece of crumpled paper. A small corner had been torn off, probably during the struggle. It was a handwritten letter, in English. The paper was of heavy stock and at the top there was a seal with an inscription under it.

" 'House of Commons'," Berrichon read slowly in a heavy French accent. "That's their parliament, isn't it?"

Sauvageot nodded.

London, May 16th
My dear Manoli:
 The bearer of this letter is one of my closest friends. She is a wonderful girl who has done a great deal for me. I commend her to you with all my heart. If I'm not mistaken, you are leaving tonight or tomorrow for a cruise in the Adriatic. May I ask you a personal favor? Take my friend with you, to taste something of the good life. She is in urgent need of rest.
                    I won't forget this service, my dear Manoli.
                    As always, devotedly yours,
                         Stanley.

The inspector read and reread the letter.

"Well, that explains everything. Naturally she didn't want to give up this letter. 'One of the closest friends' of a British Member of Parliament, eh? I always thought the English were cold fish, but apparently there's some activity on that side of the Channel too." Then, turning serious, he added, "You can let her go, but see that she stays in town until the end of the investigation. I'll send a Telex to London tonight, with a copy to Paris. We'd better keep the Minister of the Interior up to date."

Sauvageot nodded and went down to the saloon. The inspector glanced around him. The experts had finished their work. The corpse had finally been removed. Nothing remained on the deck but a dark red stain and the outline of a body drawn in chalk.

It was 4:50 in the morning when two police cars came to a screeching stop in front of the Hôtel de l'Ondine. Six detectives in plain clothes led by Inspector Berrichon leaped out and started banging on the glass doors. The night clerk — an old man in a checkered shirt — opened the door, still pulling on his pants.

Berrichon, unshaven, his eyes bloodshot, took a card from his pocket and stuck it under the clerk's sleepy eyes.

"Police!" he bellowed. "Quick! Sheila MacAlister's room!"

In his confusion, the clerk had to go through the register twice before he could find the number of the room. "Number Sixteen, Mr. Inspector. It's on the third floor — there is no elevator."

The detectives ran up the stairs. Two of them went back to the street and took up positions under Number 16's darkened window.

"Police! Open up!" Fists began pounding on the door of Number 16. "Open up!"

Berrichon strode up and down the narrow hallway. "What a mess!" he grumbled under his breath. "Jesus, what a mess!"

Barely a half hour ago, he had been awakened out of a deep sleep by a call from Paris. The private secretary to the Minister of the Interior was on the other end of the line.

"Inspector Berrichon, are you awake?" he said in an agitated voice. "Can you hear me clearly?"

"I hear you very well, sir."

"Listen, this is top-secret. You are not to repeat what I'm about to say to you to anybody — and I mean *anybody*. In response to the Telex you sent London, we have just received a telephone call from the Special Branch at Scotland Yard. They demand the immediate arrest of the MacAlister woman. A warrant for her arrest was delivered in London at 15:30 this afternoon, just after her departure for France. She is wanted for espionage, contacts with foreign agents and infractions of the Official Secrets Act. This is a very serious matter. You must arrest her immediately and hold her in solitary confinement."

Berrichon hesitated. "But, sir, this is a political crime committed in a foreign country. The person in question may ask for political asylum. I don't think it's within my powers . . ."

"I give you that power, Berrichon," the voice thundered into the receiver. "The D.S.T.* is in on it, and the Minister has given his assent. Arrest her immediately then manage to find grounds for indictment. The main thing is to get her behind bars!"

But as it turned out, Inspector Berrichon did not need to trouble about an indictment. When his men had broken in the door of Number 16 at the Hôtel de l'Ondine, they found Sheila MacAlister lying lifeless on her bed. An empty vial of Luminal lay on the floor.

* D.S.T.: Direction de la Surveillance du Territoire, the French equivalent of the F.B.I.

The inspector bent over and touched her forehead with the tips of his fingers. Her skin was cold and dry. Sheila MacAlister had been dead for several hours.

"What a mess!" Berrichon sighed, wiping his sweating face.

2

In a shabby office on the fourth floor of a rundown building behind Victoria Station, Sir Brian Auchinleck was carefully studying the report of the French police on the Theodoris-MacAlister case. When he finally finished and had closed the dossier bearing the mauve stamp of the D.S.T., he let out a deep sigh. Before him lay the proof that the most important, the most ambitious operation ever undertaken by the British Secret Service had come to nothing.

The chief of M.I.5 * looked like an outsider in Her Majesty's intelligence service. Youthful despite his forty-nine years, tall and slender, his smooth face crowned with a tuft of rebel hair, he seemed almost boyish. He habitually wore an amused smile as if he were enjoying a private joke, but his steady gaze and furrowed brow indicated otherwise. There was also the matter of his dress. His suits were always tailored in the latest style, and his colorful shirts and wide ties were the despair of his colleagues who believed that sober conservative dress was one of the important hallmarks

* M.I.5: the British counterintelligence service dealing with espionage in Britain

of a great aristocratic tradition. But they were forced to swallow this insult to Empire. For Brian Auchinleck had one of the most brilliant minds in the British Security Services.

At the end of 1971, Auchinleck was called into a meeting with the chief of the Foreign Office and the House Secretary. The British government had decided to reduce its espionage operations against the U.S.S.R. But the Russians were still expanding their activities in Britain, to the point where Her Majesty's government was becoming seriously concerned. When Sir Brian left that meeting, he had in his pocket a new assignment: Chief of M.I.5. His mission: to crack, at all costs, the Soviet spy ring in the United Kingdom.

This he was in the process of doing. In September 1971, he launched the largest operation ever undertaken by his service: the expulsion of 105 Soviet nationals employed in the Russian embassy, in trade missions and in the several import-export companies operating in London. These "trade officials" were just so many spies fishing for information in military, scientific, aeronautic and political waters. Their unorthodox occupations had been uncovered as a result of the arrest of Oleg Lyalin (which appeared fortuitous but in fact owed nothing to chance), a thirty-four-year-old employee of the London branch of Razno, a Soviet import-export firm. Lyalin turned out to be one of the principal members of the K.G.B.'s* spy ring.

Although Sir Brian had asked for the immediate expulsion of all the Russian spies, he had decided to hold on to the K.G.B.'s British agents for the time being. He had good reasons for wishing to put off their arrests: he wanted to plant his men as moles who would infiltrate their network,

* K.G.B.: the Soviet Secret Service

identify their chiefs and study their methods. Now, after an extended period of arduous work, Sir Brian was ready to deal the fatal blow to these Englishmen who had dared to betray their country.

It was at this exact moment — literally a few hours before the final showdown — that the Sheila MacAlister affair exploded, reducing all his plans to ashes.

Pen in hand, Sir Brian was about to sign the preliminary report to the Home Secretary on the Theodoris-MacAlister affair, when his young assistant, Colin Attenborough, burst into the room. Without a word, he placed the evening edition of *France-Soir* on his chief's desk.

Sir Brian looked at the bold headlines and enormous photographs with shock. Then, for the first time in many years, he lost his self-control. "Why did they have to do this? *Why?* Why couldn't the bloody idiots keep it to themselves for once?"

In point of fact, the French had not been able to keep the story secret for more than forty-one hours. *France-Soir* was first with the sensational scoop. ENGLISH MATA-HARI COMMITS SUICIDE IN SAINT-TROPEZ ran across the entire front page. And the subheads went on for several lines: "Theodoris's mysterious assassination tied to appearance of English spy on the *Anna-Maria*; Sheila MacAlister was Soviet agent; Committed suicide just before arrival of French Police; Mysterious Member of Parliament implicated in the affair."

Under the bold type were three large photographs: one of Manoli Theodoris, tanned and smiling, his arm around an unidentified beauty on board his yacht; an enlarged passport picture of Sheila MacAlister; the third and largest, a reproduction of the letter addressed to Theodoris on paper bearing the seal of the House of Commons. The caption read: "Do you recognize the handwriting?" Then: "Who is the British M.P. named Stanley? What is his last name? Why did he give the spy a personal letter of recommendation to Manoli Theodoris?"

"They can all go to hell!" Sir Brian exploded. "I begged them to give me a few days before publishing anything on this. I talked twice to de La Margerie at D.S.T., I talked to General Joilot at S.D.E.C.E.*, I talked to the Elysée. They all promised. And now look . . ."

"But don't forget that Theodoris was murdered literally under the eyes of a mob," Attenborough said.

"I don't give a damn about Theodoris's murder," Auchinleck snapped. "I'm talking about Sheila MacAlister! Here we're in the middle of making our arrests. All those who haven't been caught yet are going to destroy every document they possess. And this letter! How can we investigate what's behind this letter when it's spread across the front page of one of the biggest dailies in Europe?"

"All the same, we've got most of the network," Attenborough said. "Over fifty people. The cream of· the K.G.B.'s English agents."

"All of them except the ones we really wanted," Auchinleck said bitingly. "The ones I wanted. The ones who gave orders to Sheila MacAlister, who provided the liaison between their people and the Russians. The people coordinating the cells in Portsmouth with the Glasgow and Holy Loch people. Where the hell are *they?*"

Attenborough was silent.

Sir Brian picked up the French newspaper again. "When did it come out?" His anger was almost uncontrollable. "Why doesn't anybody tell me anything?" He pressed the

---

* S.D.E.C.E.: Service de Documentation Extérieure et de Contre-espionnage, the French equivalent of the C.I.A.

button to his intercom. "Miss Bradley, could you ask the Home Secretary if I could have an urgent word with him? . . . Yes, the Home Secretary."

"From my calculations, it's been barely an hour since the paper came out in Paris," Attenborough said evenly. He had seen the paper before his boss and had had time to work off his fury alone in his office. "Our friend at *France-Soir* succeeded in sneaking out a copy twenty minutes before they were prepared for shipment. He brought it to the airport himself. It's on the streets of Paris by now. The B.B.C. will have it on the air within a half hour."

"I suppose it's too late to get a D Notice * sent out?" Auchinleck mused.

"That's ridiculous, Brian, and you know it." A solid friendship bound the two men and Colin could afford an occasional reprimand. "Just be grateful the French haven't revealed Theodoris's real role in the affair yet."

"I suppose we lose nothing by waiting." Auchinleck's anger gave way to cynicism. "I bet we find all the details in tomorrow's papers. Ours, this time."

Attenborough looked downcast. "May I have some of your sherry?" He moved toward the bar in a corner of the room. "I'll bet you one thing," he went on, pouring himself a glass of Tio Pepe. "I bet we'll be reading a lot more than that in the morning's papers."

The telephone rang. It was Miss Bradley. "The Home Secretary is on the line, sir."

There would be no sleep for Stanley Crichton-Sloane that night.

He knew it was just a matter of hours now. Two at the

---

* In Great Britain, the government may invoke a "D Notice" to prevent the newspapers from publishing information that could compromise the country's security.

most. The time for a fast car to cover the distance between London and Haversham House in Gloucestershire. He had taken the phone off the hook at six o'clock, right after his secretary, Diana Masters, called from London to tell him about the article in *France-Soir*. In a choked voice, she had added: "The *Evening Standard* has a copy of the letter in its latest edition. I recognized your writing right away. It's you who wrote that letter, isn't it?" He hung up without answering.

He was now waiting for the reporters. They had certainly left London by now. A pack of hungry dogs baring their teeth, ready to tear him apart. Sitting in a wing chair by the fireplace where a few logs sputtered, he clasped his brandy glass. What was the meaning of the article? The incisive mind, which the *Times* of London had once described as "the ultimate hope of Her Majesty's Opposition, and perhaps of Britain herself," no longer functioned. A kind of torpor had smothered the stupefaction and rage simmering somewhere deep inside him.

Here he was, the leader of a new generation of politicians, admired by millions for his courage, his honesty, his battles for good causes in the Commons. His exploits as a fighter pilot in the R.A.F. had been extolled in books and films. His vast culture and skill in debate had propelled him to the top with dizzying speed. As Minister of State for European Affairs in the shadow cabinet, he was in line for a brilliant future.

But tonight, his luck seemed to have run out. Slumped in the chair, he stared at the flickering flames in the hearth while his wife, Jane, wandered like a ghost about the vast room. The firelight cast her shadow against the stone walls, picking out the heavy Jacobean furniture, and the portraits of ancestors, hunting rifles, swords and armor hung on the walls. Tall and majestic in her long velvet gown, the hem trailing across the faded antique rugs, her aristocratic presence was in perfect harmony with the stately manor house she had inherited from her father. Several times she had tried to approach her husband, but each time he rebuffed her in a rage which he immediately regretted. So he continued to sit motionless, gripping his glass with such force that his knuckles had turned white.

"Stan, I beg of you," Jane said at last. She approached him once again.

This time he controlled himself. "I suggest you go upstairs to bed, my dear," he said gently.

"What about you?"

"I'm going to wait." He looked at his watch. "The reporters will be here any minute now."

"I don't understand. How can you be so sure they're coming? And why should they come to you? The House of Commons must have seven or eight — "

He interrupted her brusquely. "Seven or eight members whose first name is Stanley. I know, I know. There may even be more. But it doesn't take a smart reporter more than half an hour to get specimens of their handwritings and compare them to the one on the letter. It didn't take Diana a second. Even if they didn't have samples, I can be quite sure that I have enough admirers and well-wishers to telephone all the newspapers and proclaim that of course the letter is mine."

"But you didn't write the letter. You told me that you didn't!"

He took her hand. "Do I need to tell you again? I do not know this Theodoris. I do not know this Sheila MacAlister. I've never met her. I never wrote that letter, and I swear to you that I haven't the faintest idea what it's all about."

"Then why, Stan? Why are they trying to pin it on you? I don't understand why they're doing all this." The tears she had held back so long began to run down her cheeks.

"No hysterics, Jane, please. I don't know and I don't understand. It's some kind of plot, a machination that escapes me. Somebody wants to destroy me. And that somebody has falsified my handwriting. Diana can't be wrong. She said it twice: 'It's clearly your handwriting.' "

There was a discreet cough behind their backs. Stanley started. The brandy spilled on his sleeve and ran down the arm of the leather chair.

"I didn't hear you come in, Evans," he said sharply.

"I am sorry, sir." The butler was impassive. "There are several . . . ahh . . . gentlemen who wish to see you. They say they are from the B.B.C. television, sir."

"Don't go, Stan," Jane said in a low voice. "Don't talk to them. I'll go see them. Don't take on reporters before you know the truth. They'll tear you to pieces."

Crichton-Sloane put down his glass and mechanically arranged his tie. "I can't refuse to see them," he said in a measured tone. "To avoid them would be an admission of guilt. Don't be upset, my dear. Everything will be all right."

He turned to the butler. "Please show the gentlemen into the library, Evans. This applies to any other reporters who may turn up. Tell them that I will see them in . . . let's say . . . in a half hour." He turned to Jane. "I don't want to have to do a second show for the late-comers."

At 11:30, Crichton-Sloane pushed open the double oak doors of the library and calmly walked into the room. He was blinded by flash bulbs and the intense light of the television lamps. He smiled as he raised his arm to protect his eyes. "Well, you're quite a crowd tonight, aren't you?"

The library was jammed. Thirty or forty reporters and

photographers were climbing over heirloom chairs and antique tables; scattered among them were four television crews, one of them French, and radio reporters, microphones in hand, were bent under the weight of their recording machines. The most agile of the television reporters leaped toward the door and planted himself in front of Crichton-Sloane. In one hand he held out his microphone, in the other a letter which he thrust under the Member's nose.

"Do you recognize this letter?" he said, holding the microphone up to Crichton-Sloane's mouth. The other reporters set up a chorus of questions. "Why did you write this letter to Theodoris? What was your relationship to Sheila Mac-Alister? Did you know she was a Russian agent? Are you going to resign from Parliament? What does your party think of this? Have you been interrogated by the Security Services? Have you . . ."

With a steady hand, Crichton-Sloane took the photocopy of the letter and examined it carefully, oblivious to the tumult and the exploding flash bulbs. Finally, he raised his arm and said in a low but penetrating voice, "Will you be quiet, please."

The noise subsided. Crichton-Sloane's natural magnetism and authority had their habitual effect.

"With your permission, I shall not answer your questions. I received you this evening because, in view of the news printed and broadcast during the last few hours, I have decided to make a personal statement."

He was silent for a moment, waiting politely for the television cameraman at his right to adjust his lens. "One of you has just shown me a photocopy of a letter written on House of Commons stationery, a handwritten letter signed 'Stanley.' He asked me if I recognized the letter. It is addressed

to a person named Manoli. I believe that is the late Manoli
Theodoris, and it also concerns a lady who, I have been told,
is also dead under tragic circumstances. Having examined
the letter, I can tell you that the handwriting is indeed
mine . . ."

There was an agitated murmur among the reporters. He
continued: ". . . or at least, it greatly resembles my handwriting." His voice was firm now. "I do not recognize this
letter. I have never met Mr. Manoli Theodoris, although I
have heard of him often, as have all of you, I presume. I
have never met Miss Sheila MacAlister; in fact, I never
heard of her until today. I see only one possible inference:
from the handwriting, which is a near perfect replica of
mine, and from the signature 'Stanley,' I have come to the
conclusion that I am the victim of a despicable plot aimed —
so far as I can see — at tarnishing my reputation, destroying
my family and putting an end to my political career. I have
every intention of taking bold measures, by every means at
my disposal, to bring this affair into the open and expose the
authors of this contemptible act. I need not tell you that I
am ready to cooperate fully with the police. Gentlemen, I
thank you."

In the total silence which had fallen on his audience,
Crichton-Sloane turned on his heel and left.

"I agree entirely, gentlemen, that the situation is . . . how
shall I put it . . . extremely embarrassing."

The Prime Minister fidgeted in his chair and looked quiz-
zically around the conference table. Every cabinet member
was present, except the Chancellor of the Exchequer, who
was detained in Brussels on Common Market business. The
Prime Minister resumed:

"I thank you all for coming, in view of the late hour of my

summons. I'm sure you all have an inkling of why I called this meeting. It concerns of course the role that Stanley Crichton-Sloane may have played in this matter of espionage which resulted in the death of Mr. Manoli Theodoris and Miss Sheila MacAlister at Saint-Tropez. I don't think I exaggerate when I say that the incident has aroused a great deal of anxiety throughout the country. It is for that reason that I thought it wise to invite Sir Norman Blake, in his capacity as head of the committee of the Security Services, as well as James Fleming and Sir Brian Auchinleck, of M.I.6 and M.I.5."

Seated behind the ministers at the rectangular table, Sir Brian and General Fleming responded almost imperceptibly. They were not new to meetings at 10 Downing Street.

Puffing on his pipe, the Prime Minister continued: "Sir Brian will give you a detailed report on the affair and describe a number of elements that have not yet been revealed to the general public. From information we now possess, it would appear to be even more serious than it seemed at first glance. Sir Brian, you have the floor."

The chief of M.I.5 was methodical. "You remember no doubt that in September 1971 we expelled one hundred and five Soviet agents, the list having been furnished us by a defector from the K.G.B. named Oleg Lyalin. What is not generally known is that in addition to that list Lyalin furnished us with the names of some thirty-odd British subjects who worked for the Communist espionage services. Now Lyalin knew the names of only some of the top men. Therefore it was decided not to make any immediate arrests. Instead, we gradually succeeded in planting several of our agents into various cells throughout England and Scotland, but we had not yet managed to identify the heads of the whole network. Only recently, we learned that Miss Sheila

MacAlister, an employee in the Admiralty Intelligence Department, was the principal liaison between the cell leaders and the heads of the organization. Then last week, two of our agents informed us that the network seemed to suspect that we were on their trail. That is why I decided to act immediately before the suspects could destroy their evidence and take flight. Less than an hour before we were ready to begin the arrests, Miss MacAlister succeeded in leaving England for France."

"Less than an hour before her arrest, the little bird flew out of her nest. Poem." The grating voice belonged to the Industry Secretary, James Bodley. Young and aggressive, he never missed a chance to put down the Security Services. "Your spy hunters haven't been very efficient lately, have they?"

Sir Brian ignored the challenge. He continued calmly:

"You must have asked yourselves why Miss MacAlister chose to seek refuge on board a Greek millionaire's yacht in Saint-Tropez. That is one of the few secrets" — here he gave a contrite little smile — "which the press has not yet revealed. Mr. Manoli Theodoris was generally known as an aging playboy as well as a hard-headed businessman. Actually" — Auchinleck paused for a moment and looked at the men around the table — "he was one of the principal Russian agents in Western Europe."

Bruce Updike, the Foreign Secretary, jumped up. "I don't believe it! I've known Manoli Theodoris for years. Nobody could be further from Communism than he was. This is a very serious accusation, Sir Brian. I hope you know what you are talking about."

Other expressions of disbelief erupted around the table. The Ministers' skeptical eyes converged on Auchinleck.

But he was unruffled, merely glancing at his neighbor, General Fleming, who nodded encouragement. His usual smile gone, the general looked very serious as he turned to the Foreign Secretary:

"I'm extremely sorry, Mr. Updike, but it's true. We have the information from several sources — from M.I.5 agents as well as our own. There is no longer the slightest doubt about the nature of Mr. Theodoris's clandestine activities."

"But it isn't possible," the Foreign Secretary insisted. The other cabinet members appeared to share his opinion. Why in the name of God would Theodoris become a Communist agent? It's insane!"

"I believe I can answer that," Sir Brian said. "As you pointed out, Mr. Updike, Manoli Theodoris was far from being a Communist. Quite the contrary. But he was forced into serving the K.G.B. He was their prisoner."

"Theodoris, a prisoner of the K.G.B.?" The Foreign Secretary was outraged. "What hold could the K.G.B. possibly have over a man like Theodoris?"

"Money," Sir Brian replied. "Perhaps you were not aware that in 1970 Theodoris's vast empire was on the point of collapse. He committed the unfortunate error of investing hundreds of millions of dollars in firms like I.O.S. and you know what happened to that. At the same time, Algeria and Libya nationalized their oil. That was the *coup de grâce*. He then looked into oil exploration in the North Sea. But the geography is exceedingly difficult, the weather conditions are terrible and, as a result, the test bores are very expensive. It's a long-term project which requires a great deal of staying power. Theodoris had little left and was in no position to keep investing millions. He was on the verge of having to declare bankruptcy, of losing everything he had."

The Foreign Secretary's tone changed. "Yes, I do vaguely

remember reading something about his financial difficul ties."

Sir Brian continued: "He was virtually penniless. H needed several million dollars to keep his head above wate That is where the K.G.B.'s economic department came int the picture. By setting up various fictitious corporations, th Russians bought up most of the shares in Theodoris's Euro pean operations and gave him credit at very advantageou prices. From then on, he was at their mercy. One fine da they sent him an emissary who put the cards on the table 'You have a choice: bankruptcy or collaboration with u What could he do? He gave in. We know that he had t put everything he had at the disposal of the Russians: ship ping companies, oil companies, his airline, heaven know what else . . . That is how the K.G.B. became masters of hi empire. And, financially speaking, Theodoris didn't do s badly. But by accepting their conditions, he had passed th point of no return."

"Did he actually spy for them?"

Sir Brian hesitated a moment. "Spying in the literal sens no. But he was in charge of all sorts of missions for th K.G.B. Thanks to his entrée into top military and financia circles, it was easy for him to transmit messages to Sovie networks in various countries. By the same token, he wa supposed to prospect — discreetly of course — for espio nage candidates to serve the K.G.B. You would be sur prised to know the number of highly placed men, busines tycoons, journalists and even top military officers who wer forced to work for the Russians after being photographe during a light-hearted orgy on board the *Anna-Maria* Under the guise of pleasure cruises, Theodoris's yacht wa used to take Russian agents in and out of Europe. Had h not been assassinated, he would certainly have got Sheil MacAlister safely behind the Iron Curtain."

"You realize, of course, that these revelations compound the suspicions already weighing on Crichton-Sloane," the Prime Minister noted without taking his eyes off his pipe.

"Yes, I'm well aware of that," Sir Brian replied. "But don't forget one important factor: I have no proof whatsoever. Only suspicions." Carefully weighing his words, he went on: "This is how things look as of this moment: we have every reason to fear — I know it sounds insane, but everything seems to point in that direction — that Crichton-Sloane is one of the chiefs of the Communist spy ring in Great Britain. Sheila MacAlister was undoubtedly the only person who knew this. When she found out that the network was about to be exposed and that she would be arrested, she rushed to Crichton-Sloane. He had to help her get away immediately. The case was urgent; there was no time for the usual precautions. So he writes — in his own hand — what appears to be a perfectly innocent letter to Manoli Theodoris, asking him to take her on a cruise. If you read his letter carefully, you will see that it is in fact a camouflaged command, ordering Theodoris to make an immediate getaway with Sheila MacAlister."

"Are you trying to tell us that Theodoris was under Crichton-Sloane's orders?" Bodley asked.

Sir Brian paid him no heed. "Theodoris knew who Crichton-Sloane was and all about his clandestine activities. No doubt he had often transmitted messages and instructions to him in the past. Had Theodoris not been assassinated, he would have left with Sheila MacAlister and no one would have been any the wiser. The letter would never have been discovered."

"Who killed Theodoris?" Sir Emory Browning, the Defense Minister, asked peremptorily.

"I haven't the faintest idea. Possibly one of the Security Services in the West decided to liquidate him after discovering what he was up to. Maybe the French. Their *action-service,* which functions inside the S.D.E.C.E., specializes in just this kind of violent operation."

"Why should they be interested in this sort of assassination?" Sir Emory asked.

General Fleming intervened. "It could just as well be the Russians. The K.G.B. may have learned that we were about to expose their British network. They might also have known — through a double agent — that we were onto Theodoris, and that if we got our hands on him, it would be all over for them — and perhaps in Western Europe as well. Theodoris knew too many of their agents. So, the K.G.B. decides to get rid of him and dispatches a band of killers to Saint-Tropez. At the same moment, Crichton-Sloane happens to send Sheila MacAlister to Theodoris. The Russians certainly weren't going to warn Crichton-Sloane that they were about to kill Theodoris, and Crichton-Sloane had no way of warning them that the Greek was going to ferry Sheila MacAlister to safety. Just lack of coordination, that's all."

The Lord Chancellor had seemed to be dozing, indifferent to the charged atmosphere around him. Now he came to and slowly leaned forward. "Do you have any solid proof against Crichton-Sloane?"

"Only the letter, sir," Sir Brian replied.

"But he claims he didn't write it."

Sir Brian shrugged. "I know. And even if I find a handwriting expert to prove in court that he was the author, the defense will find ten more to prove it's a fake."

"Is that a real possibility? That it's a fake?"

"Theoretically, yes, but I don't believe it. I would rather not give a definitive judgment at this point, but everything would seem to indicate that Crichton-Sloane is our man. It is true that he denies writing the letter, but his denials are not very convincing. Every newspaper, without exception, is skeptical. They all want his hide. When they find out that Theodoris was also a Russian agent, they'll lynch Crichton-Sloane."

The Defense Secretary interrupted. "You mentioned litigation. What about his parliamentary status?"

"There will be no problem there, sir. Crichton-Sloane called us this morning to say he would volunteer to submit to interrogation. He says he will take all steps to prove his innocence . . ."

An earnest young man entered the room on tiptoe and placed a note in front of the Prime Minister. Shifting his gaze from the smoke rings he had been blowing to the note, the P.M. cleared his throat. "Excuse me, gentlemen. I have just been informed that some members of our party and two members of the Opposition are prepared to call us to account over the accusations against Crichton-Sloane. Her Majesty's Government must follow a very strict line of conduct in this matter."

"If you will allow me . . ." This was John Baldwin, the Employment Minister, and chairman of the party. Small and pugnacious, he owed his portfolio to his political power far more than to his administrative competence. His political instincts were almost infallible.

"Let us assume that there is one chance in a thousand that Crichton-Sloane did not write this wretched letter. In that case we'd look like a pack of fools. We musn't forget his extraordinarily powerful position in the country, that he is one of the leaders of the Opposition. And this is an election year. If we do not succeed in proving his guilt beyond the shadow of a doubt, the whole affair could become counterproductive. Public opinion always sides with the victim. This is a very, very delicate matter."

"Yes," the Prime Minister agreed. "It is indeed a very del-

icate situation. That is why I suggest that, for the time
being, the government refrain from any official reaction.
We will tell the press that the affair is in the hands of the
S.I.S. At the same time, we should not publish any information about Theodoris's real role in the affair."

"In that case, what am I supposed to do about Crichton-
Sloane?" Sir Brian asked irritably. The intrusion of party
politics into matters involving national security always annoyed him.

The Prime Minister was brusque. "Take him at his word.
Have him submit to an interrogation. I want a complete
dossier on him — everything you can lay your hands on.
And please keep me informed daily on the progress of the
interrogation."

Auchinleck and Fleming took care not to be seen leaving
10 Downing Street. They went out via Number 11 and, as
they emerged, they could hear the commotion down the
street when the first wave of reporters confronted the ministers leaving Number 10.

The muffled telephone bell sounded at two in the morning in the bedroom of Sir Brian's Mayfair apartment. As
always when his wife, Eleanor, wasn't there — she was visiting her mother in Sussex — he was sleeping fitfully. He
picked up the receiver.

"Yes?" he mumbled.

General Fleming was at the other end.

"Brian, have you seen the morning newspapers?"

Sir Brian was curt. "No. I don't usually read the papers
at two o'clock in the . . ."

"Look, I'm not joking." Fleming was not only agitated but
embarrassed. "They've just brought them to me from the
office. I thought you ought to know that the whole Theo-

doris business is out, in banner headlines, down to the last detail."

"What on earth do you mean?"

"Just what I said. The whole story: Theodoris victimized by the K.G.B., the financial transactions, his turning Russian agent, courier, procurer of spies — the whole story. Every single detail."

Auchinleck tried to organize his thoughts. "But who gave them the story?"

He heard what sounded like a snort at the other end of the line. "Who? You'll never get him to admit it, but I'll bet you anything it's that foxy old Employment Minister, Baldwin. Remember how worried he was about the effect on the elections? . . ."

"Yes, he was the one in the cabinet who wanted us to play it down."

"Right. But he couldn't care less if the press tears Crichton-Sloane to pieces. As long as the government isn't off on a witch hunt — and the press is very clear on that — there's nothing he'd like better than to set the press against the Opposition. After all, what a windfall, just before a general election!"

"I really don't like all this politicking," Auchinleck said with a sigh, adding "but I wouldn't want to be in Crichton-Sloane's shoes."

There was a brief silence. Then Fleming said, "Actually, I wasn't calling you about the newspapers. Something happened tonight that's much more surprising and far more serious."

"What's that, for God's sake?"

"It's on the same subject — Theodoris and Crichton-Sloane. I'd like you to come over right now. I have somebody here who wants to tell you something."

"Now? At this time of night? Surely it can wait."

"It cannot. Please, come right away. And for heaven's sake, be careful. You know my service entrance on Lancaster Gate? Miles will be waiting for you there. You'll come right away?"

"Yes, of course," Auchinleck replied with only the briefest hesitation. Fleming had never asked to see him at this hour of the night before. That the chief of M.I.6 should have to forgo a night's sleep could only mean that there was something very, very unusual afoot.

It was seven in the morning when Sir Brian left General Fleming's house. He looked stunned. With trembling fingers he searched in his pocket for his car key and finally managed to insert it in the keyhole of his black Bentley. When he had slid behind the wheel, he closed his eyes and said out loud:

"I don't believe it. I don't believe it."

3

THE NOCTURNAL MEETING between the two chiefs of the Security Services marked a dramatic turning point in the course of the investigation. But this time there were no leaks to the papers.

In the Sunday press, on television, on the radio, the storm over the affair continued to rage. Photographs of Crichton-Sloane filled the front pages. His life, his political career, his opinions, his habits, his favorite hobbies were described in minute detail. As for his private life — his early years of struggle, his marriage to the aristocratic Jane Haversham, their children, the manor house in Gloucestershire — nothing was left out.

But the bloodhounds of the press had no way of knowing that at the exact same moment, the Crichton-Sloane affair had galloped off in an entirely different direction. When he had left General Fleming, Sir Brian immediately telephoned the Prime Minister. The call had unleashed the most frantic activity at the highest levels. At eleven o'clock that morning, the two men met at Chequers. The key cabinet members had again been summoned posthaste. Once assembled, they listened to the top-secret report of the chiefs of Security Services. A second secret meeting took place the following morning, with the addition of some unidentified men who arrived in a limousine with its shades drawn. A stack of coded telegrams marked "Top-Secret — Personal — Destroy after reading" had been exchanged between General Fleming and a minor attaché at the British embassy in Moscow, who was employed — at least officially — as embassy archivist. That same evening, the counterintelligence service delivered to the Prime Minister an urgent report on one Ephraim Kolodni, the assistant director of a Soviet importing firm called Sovchim. Kolodni had spent two days in England — May 15 and 16 — in order to buy a patent from the British firm, Royal Oil.

That same Sunday, Stanley Crichton-Sloane, back in his town house in Belgravia, received a curious telephone call from Colin Attenborough. Sir Brian's assistant informed him that his interrogation by the S.I.S. had been postponed. No, he could not give the new date. The M.P. put down the receiver with an expression of surprise not untinged with hope.

Monday started much like the preceding days: headlines in the papers, photographs of Crichton-Sloane, articles on how the rest of the world was taking the scandal. But, a little after twelve, the sensitive antennae of the British press picked up the first sign of a sudden turnabout. In answer to a question at a press conference, the spokesman for the Home Office said, "The press reports which assert that Her Majesty's Government suspects Mr. Crichton-Sloane of any unlawful deeds are without foundation. Nor have I any information about any plan that he submit to an interrogation."

The reporters were stunned.

At three in the afternoon, the Foreign Secretary issued a communiqué in which he stated: "Sir Norman Blake, Under-Secretary of State for Foreign Affairs, has informed Mr. Ivan Abrassimov, chargé d'affaires at the Soviet embassy, that henceforth Mr. Ephraim Kolodni of the Russian firm Sovchim will be considered *persona non grata* in the United Kingdom. During his stay in Great Britain, Mr. Kolodni took part in activities detrimental to the security of the country, establishing contact with Miss Sheila MacAlister, since deceased. This activity is contrary to the commitments made by Mr. Andrei Gromyko, Minister of Foreign Affairs of the U.S.S.R., during the course of meetings held in London in October 1970 and in Moscow in December 1972, with Her Majesty's Government's then Foreign Secretary, Sir Alec Douglas-Home."

A third statement was released that same evening by the Home Office. It was a bombshell. "At 17:15, the Special Brigade of Scotland Yard arrested Mr. Dennis Egleton, fifty-five, the representative of British Chemicals Ltd. in Moscow. At the end of last week, Mr. Egleton made a business trip to Geneva, and was called back to London on receipt of a telegram from his firm. He arrived at Heathrow this morning at 11:45. By order of the Home Secretary, he was apprehended upon arrival and interrogated by officers of Scotland Yard's Special Brigade. As a result of the interrogation, Mr. Egleton was duly arrested. Mr. Egleton is suspected of threatening the security of the kingdom. He is cooperating fully with his interrogators."

By eleven-thirty that night, the last news broadcaster on Radio Four was able to announce: "Authorized sources state that Mr. Dennis Egleton is implicated in the Theodoris-MacAlister affair. His deposition appears to have provided the Security Services with the key to the enigma surrounding the letter attributed to Mr. Crichton-Sloane. They add that his confession removes all traces of suspicion relative to the M.P. Dennis Egleton will be tried on charges of espionage on behalf of the U.S.S.R. Preliminary hearings will take place shortly. As for Mr. Crichton-Sloane, he was seen tonight at a West End restaurant, celebrating the event with a group of friends."

On the other side of the Atlantic, in the Oval Room of the White House, the President of the United States picked up his telephone: "The Director of the C.I.A., please."

A Bell 206 helicopter skimmed the tops of the pine trees of Langley Forest in Virginia. The pilot glanced down at the Potomac, winding its silvery way on his left. Across the river, the spring sun cast a shimmering light on the immaculate Capitol, the Washington Monument and the imposing Kennedy Center. The craft then peeled away from the superhighway it had been following, flew directly over a secondary road and turned gracefully toward a block of buildings surrounded by parking lots and a double fence. From a distance, the complex looked like the administrative offices of a large industrial or business concern. Any automobile that inadvertently found itself on the road leading to the complex would have ended up before a modest sign which read "Study Center for Fairbank Highway Research Station." But the fifteen thousand employees working in the barricaded offices in the heart of the forest knew next to nothing about transportation and toll roads. They worked in the greatest espionage center in the world, the headquarters of the Central Intelligence Agency.

The helicopter landed on a large asphalt strip near the building's north wing. Four guards armed with submachine guns stood at the edges of the strip, fingers on the trigger,

heir eyes on the aircraft. The helicopter's sole passenger
lidn't even seem to notice them. He was busy pinning his
dentity card, with colored photograph, name and signature,
•nto the lapel of his jacket. Then he gathered up the
•apers on his lap, murmured some words of thanks to the
•ilot and jumped to the ground. Obeying an automatic re-
lex, he lowered his head as he passed under the still whirl-
ng blades of the helicopter and ran between the sentries
•osted at the entrance to the north wing. The guards made
10 motion to stop him. A glance at his identity card told
hem that he was one of the heads of the Operational Divi-
ion of the C.I.A.

"Mr. Jeff Saunders." The security officer on duty at the
loor examined the new arrival who pulled a tin box from
iis pocket and extracted a black panatela. The trained eye
•f the officer measured and classified the man standing in
ront of him: six foot one, about thirty-five, lithe, loose-
ointed, in good physical condition. Tanned face and hands,
rademark of the outdoor man. Thick brown hair, broad
orehead, strong chin, the facial expression both composed
ind energetic. Not the sort you'd want to tangle with, the
•fficer said to himself.

He looked once again at the papers in his right hand and
onsulted the list in his left.

"Yes, you are expected, sir. Please follow me."

Jeff Saunders lit his cigarillo and removed his dark
;lasses, revealing lively blue eyes which contrasted sharply
vith the severity of his other features. He set off after a
;uard who had appeared from nowhere, and followed him
lown the endless halls of the building.

Three times they were stopped by different security con-
rols, but Saunders was not asked to show his papers. His
dentity card satisfied them as well as the closed-circuit televi-

sion cameras focused on his face. The last control guarded
the elevator.

"Jeff Saunders, for the Director," the guard said to the security officer and turned on his heels.

The officer nodded and addressed Jeff. "Will you step inside the elevator please, sir."

The elevator went directly to the offices of the Director.
Jim Sullivan was waiting by the elevator doors, a large smile
on his broad face. "Welcome, Jeff. Sorry about the obstacle
course." The chief of the C.I.A. and Jeff Saunders were old
friends. During the previous chief's tenure, they had both
taken part in one of the most difficult operations in the
agency's history.

"How are things on the Farm *?" Sullivan said, pouring a
double Scotch for his colleague. He himself didn't drink.

"O.K.," Saunders said with a grin. "It was just what I
needed. After all that paperwork you've been giving me, I
was in lousy shape."

Sullivan's attention was elsewhere. "What do you think
about all that?" he asked, pointing to the pile of English
newspapers Saunders had placed on his desk.

"It's a strange business. I'm afraid I don't get it, Jim."

"You're not the only one," and Sullivan opened a blue
dossier lying on the desk. "The report from our correspondent in London leaves a lot of questions unanswered.
Taken separately, each of the stories seems plausible
enough. I can explain Theodoris's assassination, Sheila Mac-
Alister's suicide, even the arrest of that man Egleton —
Dennis Egleton. Each link in the chain has a certain logic.

---

* The Farm: The name given by the C.I.A. operatives to their secret training camp on the East Coast. There, agents about to be sent on missions are
initiated into the techniques of espionage: codes, drops, recruitment of
agents, weaponry, sabotage, sidearms, hand-to-hand combat, etc.

But put them together . . . Then that letter that was or wasn't written by a Member of Parliament. The whole thing is pretty weird."

Jeff said nothing, content to let his boss try to unravel the plot.

"I had a lot of trouble explaining the thing to the President yesterday. He's very concerned, you know. He'd met Theodoris several times. But he also knew Crichton-Sloane from way back when he was a senator. Not to mention the fact that it's an election year in England and Crichton-Sloane is a leading member of the shadow cabinet. Their next Prime Minister, possibly. The whole thing could have important repercussions."

"I don't see why it concerns us," Jeff said. "It's strictly a British affair."

Sullivan thought a moment before answering.

"Jeff, do you know about the 'Crown Project'?"

Saunders frowned. " 'Crown'? Isn't that something to do with extending the ABM network beyond our borders? I seem to remember reading a Blue Circular about it."

Sullivan nodded. "Right. The 'Crown Project' is the code name for the English proposal that we furnish them twenty-five multiple-head ABM rockets. The Goliaths. You know the Goliath — top-secret, the latest model. Up to now, we've refused to let it out of the country, but lately the English have been putting a lot of pressure on the Administration. They feel very vulnerable to a nuclear attack from the U.S.S.R. They've lost all faith in NATO, all faith in the European Defense Community. If we give them our Goliaths, they appear willing in return to intervene with their nuclear arsenal in case of a Russian attack on the U.S. That's very important to us. We know the Russians' rockets are trained on our ICBM bases. If war broke out, they could wipe most

of them out. But if they have to face simultaneous attack
from England and us, they'll find themselves in a very tight
spot."

"So we're ready to trust the English with our latest secret
weapons? I don't like that at all."

"That's just it. A lot of people don't. The President could
do it. But he'd run into a lot of obstacles. The Foreign
Relations Committee and the Armed Forces Committee in
the Senate, for one thing. And you know Mel Ryan, the
Kansas senator. He's determined to do everything he can to
wreck the project. His selling point is that we can't trust a
country that's infested with Soviet spies. If we go through
with 'Crown,' he says, in a matter of weeks, or at most a few
months, all our strategic secrets will be in the hands of the
Russians."

"And this Crichton-Sloane business . . ."

"And this Crichton-Sloane business can bury the whole
'Crown Project' for all time. If it's really as serious as it
looks, the President will have to give up on it. That's why
we want to know — before we go any further — just exactly
what happened."

"Is that a wish or a command?"

Sullivan smiled. "I want you to go to London. I know
that paperwork bores you to death. You're too young for it.
And you can't spend your life torturing my judo instructors
on the Farm. Go to London and see if you can make any
sense out of this."

Saunders showed little eagerness. "Since when do we conduct secret operations in England?"

"This is no secret operation," Sullivan said with some as-
perity. "This is a perfectly legitimate mission. Now get
going. Egleton's hearing starts next week."

"Next week! Why so early? What's their hurry?"

"That's what I'd like to know. In any case, I want you to follow the trial. Listen, observe, then write me a report."

"What if it's held *in camera*?"

"You'd be allowed into the courtroom anyway. After all, Brian Auchinleck is an old pal of yours, from back when he represented British intelligence here in Washington."

Saunders was still unenthusiastic. His chief gave him an affectionate pat.

"Look, I know. You've had more interesting assignments. Why don't you look at it as a paid vacation."

"O.K., boss," Saunders gave him a thin smile and walked out the door.

As he stretched out in the limousine taking him back to Washington, he thought of the many times — at noon, at midnight, in snow and rain, or even on a beautiful sunny day like this one — he had left that awesome building and set out on a new mission. The circumstances had varied, the assignments had been different. But there was one constant. He was always alone. For he was a lone wolf who hated working with a team; he had confidence only in himself. He avoided other agents, refusing to include them either in his calculations or in his maneuvers. His friends, colleagues and superiors sometimes accused him of arrogance and a certain recklessness. Little did they know what self-doubts, what paralyzing fear gripped him each time he started on a new mission. The secret war was fought with its own implacable rules: double and triple betrayals, intrigues, machinations, lies and abuse. He wanted to play the game according to his own rules. And if he met his match one day, it would be his own damn fault.

That was how he had played his cards during the Cuban missile crisis in 1962. Using a false French identity (which wasn't too far off the mark, for his mother was French and had taken great pains to see that he spoke the language faultlessly), he spent two months in Cuba where he succeeded in gaining access to the port of Santiago and photographed the clandestine unloading of Soviet equipment. The experts in Washington were able to establish that the cargo involved parts for Soviet missile launching installations. It was this discovery that started Washington off on the right track.

Still alone, Saunders had found himself later that year in Saint-Malo where he and three Breton sailors set off on a winter fishing expedition into the North Sea. It hadn't taken him long to pick up the peculiar accent and idioms of Brittany. The small trawler had slowly made its way to the icy waters off the Faroe Islands, where NATO maintained a secret submarine base. In the distance, he could just make out a Soviet fishing fleet circling the islands. He knew perfectly well what the Russians hoped to catch in their nets. He could guess what their cameras were aimed at, and their radar, and the hypersensitive electronic instruments hidden in their holds. One evening, he slipped into a frogman's black rubber suit and strapped bottles of compressed air on his back. But instead of the usual lead weights, he had a heavy and sinister-looking black object attached to his chest. When the bomb exploded and the Soviet trawler flew into a thousand pieces, the Saint-Malo fishermen were already on their way back to their home port. Being good listeners, Moscow got the message.

Again, in 1964, in a dark alley leading to the Berlin Wall, he picked up C.I.A. agent Rand Hodges as he was about to defect. Three years later, he was in the Middle East just before the outbreak of the Six Day War. Two years after that, he engineered the escape of the chief of the Czech

Secret Services, an abortive operation which cost the life of his old colleague and friend, Elmer Connally. Then, more recently, there was that stormy night when he set out to solve the mysterious assassination of the Soviet Foreign Minister, Lev Ponomarev, and found out far more than he had been asked to.

He had few illusions left. Today, he felt none of the emotional intoxication, the fear, the anticipation that used to come over him on the eve of a new mission. This was errand boy's work. Sullivan had said it: "Go to London; listen, observe and write me a report."

He threw the butt of his cigarillo out the car window, glanced through the papers on his lap and perfunctorily examined the photograph of the British spy, Dennis Egleton.

Tall and desiccated, Dennis Harold Egleton stood before the judge. He was a middle-aged, stoop-shouldered man with sparse colorless hair parted to one side. His clothes were baggy and worn. He stood in the witness stand, thin-lipped and steely-eyed, seemingly unaware of the excited crowd jostling for places in Courtroom Number 7 of the Old Bailey, or the many curious eyes focused on him.

Jeff Saunders watched from his seat near a vaulted window. It was a typical June morning. Although it was almost summer, a gray sky hung over the city and gusts of wind splattered raindrops against the windows. It had been like this for two days, from the moment Jeff landed at Heathrow and made for the apartment the service had rented for him in Kensington. Sir Brian Auchinleck had greeted him with restrained enthusiasm. He seemed disturbed, and when they dined together at his club, the Somerset, he brushed aside every question Jeff put to him. His constant refrain was "Let's leave that until the hearing begins." The case ob-

viously worried him. "I can't stand working under spot-
lights," he said during one of the few moments of their
former intimacy. "All this publicity has made the last weeks
a nightmare." Jeff was surprised to learn that the trial was
to be in public. "At least the first part," Sir Brian had said.
"Egleton has decided to confess. He knows he's washed up
with the Russians. All that interests him now is getting out
with the shortest possible sentence."

"Yes, but why a public trial?" Saunders asked.

"Because the trial is of the greatest public significance.
Crichton-Sloane's name has been dragged through the
mud — because of that damn letter, he is considered a traitor and a spy. One thing is certain: Egleton is in a position
to clear him of all suspicion. The M.P. still has a brilliant future before him. He has been publicly defamed, and therefore he must be publicly rehabilitated. People won't believe
his innocence unless we provide them with tangible proof.
Which means a public trial, everything out in the open, and,
above all, Egleton's complete and detailed confession."

"And he's ready to confess?"

"Yes."

Jeff was still not satisfied. "In other words, you've made
a deal. With the cooperation of the prosecution, I imagine."

"Call it what you will," Sir Brian said evasively. "As for
the trial, we may ask to move it *in camera* for the second part,
the part that concerns operational secrets, the more — shall
I say — delicate aspects of the case. But everything bearing
on Crichton-Sloane will take place in public. You'll see for
yourself."

Which was what Saunders was doing. The judge, Mr. Justice Maudling, called for order in the court, and the prosecution summoned a series of witnesses whose depositions

were purely technical. Then it was the turn of counsel for the defense. Leaning deferentially toward the judge, he said, "M'lud, the defense will call only one witness."

Dennis Egleton took his place in the dock and was sworn in.

"Your name, occupation, date and place of birth, please."

The witness spoke in a clear firm voice. "Dennis Harold Egleton, born in Lewes, Sussex, on December 4, 1918."

"What is your profession, Mr. Egleton?"

"I am a businessman. I represent British Chemicals Limited in Moscow."

Question followed question, dry, precise, informative. It was quite obvious that the barrister was making no attempt to establish a line of defense for his client. Jeff's hypothesis seemed confirmed: Egleton would confess his guilt, he would expose every detail of the affair in order completely to exonerate Crichton-Sloane. The judge, in turn, would give him the lightest possible sentence.

When the prosecuting counsel rose to his feet, Jeff was not surprised to see that he had guessed right. The counsel wasted no time on preliminary questions.

"You were involved in clandestine activities for the Russian espionage services, Mr. Egleton, is that correct?"

Jeff glanced quickly at the defense counsel. He hadn't batted an eye.

"Yes," Egleton answered without the slightest hesitation.

"Would you tell us exactly when you began your activities for the Russians?"

"In 1953, after the election of General Eisenhower as President of the United States. It was my belief that the results of that election threatened the peace of the world."

"Your motives were therefore purely ideological?"

"Yes, sir."

"All the same, you received substantial sums of money from the Soviets, did you not?"

For the first time, Egleton hesitated for a fraction of a second. "Yes," he said finally. "On a few occasions."

"Would you describe for us the nature of your activities on behalf of the K.G.B. while you were in England?"

Egleton embarked on a long recital of his activities. He told how, on his own initiative, he had entered into contact with the naval attaché to the Russian embassy during the period when he was the principal supplier of electronic matériel to the British Navy; how he was put in charge of various espionage missions by different departments at the Russian embassy, by the Soviet trade delegation and several Soviet export-import firms operating in London. He ticked off a list of dates, of rendezvous, of names and letter drops; he described how he made contacts, the code names used and the location of dead-letter boxes. He told how, at different stages, he had recruited four other Englishmen for the spy network, and how his activities increased in scope when he became one of the principal suppliers to the British Army and the NATO naval units stationed in Britain. He also mentioned how, after 1955, he visited the Soviet Union and other countries in the Communist bloc under the guise of effecting commercial transactions.

Jeff listened with one ear. Most of this information was all too familiar, without interest or value where this case was concerned. But his ears pricked up when Egleton mentioned the name of Colonel Ramsey Collier, former chief of the Soviet section in the R.A.F.'s Second Bureau. Egleton reminded his listeners how Collier had been the K.G.B.'s *bête noire* in Britain, especially when, on leaving the army, he had launched a crusade against Soviet espionage in England, denouncing the nest of spies that functioned out of the embassy and the Russian trade delegation in London. It was this program which had won Collier his election to the House of Commons where he continued his campaign against the Russians. Egleton's contact during this period was an employee of Aeroflot named Razumov who asked him what could be done to destroy Collier. Egleton submitted to the Russians a detailed plan of action. When Collier subsequently made a trip to Moscow with a group from the House of Commons, it happened that the guide furnished by Intourist was a ravishing blonde by the name of Ludmilla Arbatova. She was also a young lady who apparently couldn't say "no." So Collier returned to London, his heart overflowing with memories of delicious nights of love. The Russians also benefited from the Englishman's nocturnal pleasures. A few months before the elections of 1967, they circulated a number of titillating photographs showing Ramsey Collier making love with blond Ludmilla. The M.P. lost his seat, his wife and his work, while Egleton's prestige in Russian eyes rose to new heights. When he arrived in Moscow in 1968, as the representative of British Chemicals in the Soviet Union, Egleton soon found himself the semiofficial counselor to the chiefs of the psychological warfare division in charge of all matters concerning England.

"It was at Anatole Blagomirov's — he was head of the division — that we first discussed the problem of Stanley Crichton-Sloane," Egleton said with no change in his voice. "About six months ago, Blagomirov summoned me to a meeting at the offices of Sovchim. Ephraim Kolodni, my contact at this time, was also present. The Russians said that Crichton-Sloane was beginning to worry them. His personality, his leadership qualities were bound to put him in a position of influence if his party came to power. Everyone knew of his profound aversion to Communism and the Soviet Union. The general election was approaching. It was therefore important to eliminate Crichton-Sloane as soon as possible, especially since he had already assumed Collier's place as leader of the professional anti-Communists in Parliament. If he were appointed a cabinet minister after the elections, there might well be a fundamental change for the worse in Britain's relations with the U.S.S.R.

"They asked me to come forward with a plan that would end Crichton-Sloane's career." Egleton's voice continued on an even tone, without a trace of emotion. "I proposed that we undermine his prestige by tarnishing his private life. We would repeat 'operation Ludmilla' which had worked so well with Ramsey Collier. We did in fact set traps for Crichton-Sloane on two different occasions, once when he was visiting Geneva, another time in Helsinki. But both times he seemed unmoved by the charms of the young ladies we provided.

"On May 14th, I was again summoned to the offices of Sovchim and was taken from there to K.G.B. headquarters on Djerdjinski Square, in that part of the building that overlooks Lubyanka Prison. The meeting was held in the office of the chief of psychological warfare, and several K.G.B. officials were there, all in a state of considerable agitation.

"The chief announced that something very serious had just happened in England. It appeared that British agents had managed to uncover the K.G.B.'s spy network and that a series of arrests would be taking place within the next few days. He also said that the English had apparently found out all about Manoli Theodoris's clandestine activities. This meant that his usefulness had come to an end."

The prosecuting counsel interrupted. "Did they use the term 'come to an end'?"

"Yes," Egleton said without hesitation. "I must confess I didn't take in the full meaning of the phrase at the time. But after what happened in Saint-Tropez on May 16th, I understood."

"You therefore think it was the Russians themselves who assassinated Theodoris?"

This question irritated the judge. Mr. Justice Maudling gave the prosecution a withering look. "We are not here to listen to conjectures from the accused. Please stick to the facts. Continue, if you please."

Egleton gave a faint smile. "I apologize, M'lud. At that very same meeting, one of the K.G.B. men — I didn't know him — said to me; 'Our whole British network may be on the verge of collapse. But perhaps we can gain something by it. We could try to bring Crichton-Sloane down in the general shambles.' "

A murmur of surprise swept through the courtroom.

"Those were his very words," Egleton went on. " 'Bring Crichton-Sloane down in the general shambles.' "

"Did they have a plan?" the prosecution asked.

Egleton paused for a moment. "Yes, they had several. But I had the distinct impression that it was all done in a very great hurry, as if they were improvising *in extremis.* One of the men responsible for espionage in Great Britain may have felt his position jeopardized by the general collapse and so decided to save his skin by counterattacking, going after Crichton-Sloane. I must admit I was astonished, because the K.G.B. is not given to doing things in a hurry. In fact, they are usually very slow. It's the Russian mentality."

There was a ripple of laughter in the room.

"May we stick to the facts, please?" This time it was the prosecuting counsel who was showing signs of impatience. "Why did they call on you? What did you think you could do?"

"They told me they had specimens of Crichton-Sloane's handwriting. They asked me to compose three different texts as if they had been written by him. Obviously, texts that would incriminate him if they were published. So I wrote up the three texts, and they were taken to their counterfeiting laboratories. I had no idea which one they would use, or when or in what circumstances. None of them was dated."

"What were the contents of the three documents?" the prosecutor asked. There was visible tension in the room now.

"The first was a report on various attitudes toward the Soviet Union in the House of Commons. The second was a letter addressed to an agent at Holy Loch asking for information about some new installations at the atomic submarines base. As for the third — " Egleton paused for a moment, clearly enjoying the situation — "the third was a letter asking Manoli Theodoris to take a certain passenger on board his yacht, the *Anna-Maria*."

The reaction was immediate. The audience was stunned, while the prosecution jumped to his feet and waved a sheet of paper at the judge.

"I ask M'lud to enter this as Exhibit A." The judge nodded, and immediately buried his head in his papers.

The prosecuting counsel continued: "Mr. Egleton, do you recognize this document?"

Egleton read the letter carefully. "Yes, it's one of the texts I prepared at K.G.B. headquarters on the 14th of May. It was copied by hand on a House of Commons letterhead and dated May 16th. The text is identical to the one I composed."

With a theatrical flourish, the prosecution turned to the judge. "M'lud, the letter just now identified by the accused is the very same letter that has been attributed to Stanley Crichton-Sloane!"

The courtroom was in a furor. Eager reporters elbowed

their way to the telephones to transmit the sensational news to their editors. In the commotion, Jeff Saunders took in two faces: one, the crimson face of the judge banging his gavel to try to bring the court to order; the other, that of Ron Bates, chief of U.P.I.'s London bureau, the veins in his neck distended, calling out to his colleague posted by the exit: "Transmit: 'The Crichton-Sloane letter a K.G.B. hoax!' "

Then it was Jeff's turn to get up and thread his way through the crowd toward the exit.

Sir Brian shifted in his chair. He was clearly ill at ease. "Please, Jeff, let's not talk about operational matters . . ." Then he thought better of it and continued, choosing his words carefully. "We found out that Ephraim Kolodni had arrived in London on May 15th and had seen Sheila Mac-Alister. My men also established the fact that he was the only Russian she knew.

"The moment we knew whom we were dealing with, our next move became clear. We found out that Kolodni was in constant touch with Dennis Egleton in Moscow. So we devised a fairly complicated operation. At our behest, the deputy director at British Chemicals took a plane for Geneva where he telephoned Egleton, telling him that within the next twenty-four hours he was to sign a contract with representatives from Communist China for the building of a plastics factory. It was absolutely essential that they discuss the matter before the signing because it would mean delaying several projects British Chemicals had under consideration with the Russians. Since the negotiations would be taking place in Geneva, it would facilitate matters if Egleton could join them there. This Egleton did. But on arrival he found a message telling him that, at the last minute, the Chinese had decided to visit a British Chemicals factory in Bristol, and would he please meet them there. So he did that too. I don't know if he was beginning to suspect anything, but so far as we were concerned, the main thing was that we had gotten him out of the Soviet Union."

"But how could you be so sure he was the one?" Jeff asked.

"To tell the truth, I wasn't sure at all. What I really wanted was to get him to talk to us about Kolodni. But he went to pieces as soon as he arrived at the airport. He seemed terribly tense. First he denied having seen Kolodni recently. Then he changed his story. He said he didn't know Kolodni had come to London. He couldn't know that our informant at the Moscow embassy had given us detailed reports about their meetings during the preceding days. His answers aroused our suspicions. We began to tighten the screws a little. He broke down when I told him he was up to his neck in a thoroughly nasty business and that if I let him go, the Russians would be convinced he had talked and would finish him off on the spot. That was all he needed. He agreed to confess, on condition that we would protect him and make every effort to get him a light sentence."

"Do you think you'll bring it off?"

Sir Brian shrugged. "All we can do is hope. You know British justice. The judge will decide. All we can do is put in a plea in mitigation."

"But the trial has several more days to run," Jeff said.

"Yes, I know." Sir Brian got up and started to usher Saunders to the door. "Now we have other things to attend to. At least the Crichton-Sloane case is finished."

But the Crichton-Sloane case was far from finished. Three days later, it took a quite unexpected turn.

Jeff was sitting in his usual seat at the Old Bailey facing the dock. The room was half empty. After the first day's bombshell, the crowd had begun to thin out. Overnight, Crichton-Sloane had become a national hero. The press couldn't say enough about his noble attitude, his courage under fire. The newspaper columns were full of touching tales about the return of happy days in the family mansion. The spy who with one stroke of the pen had almost reduced the brilliant politician's career to ashes was not able to attract more than a handful of spectators.

It all happened in the middle of the prosecution's charge. Facing the judge, his back turned to Egleton, the counsel had just started to inveigh against the black soul and vile treachery of the accused. Aren't they pushing it a little, after what they promised Egleton? Jeff said to himself and turned to see how the accused was taking it. What he saw made him start. Egleton had just slumped in his chair, his chest heaving, his forehead covered with sweat, his face a deathly bluish gray. He was clawing at his shirt collar with trembling fingers, his mouth opening and shutting in spasms.

"Help him! Help him, quick!" One of the courtroom police had taken in Egleton's condition and interrupted the counsel. "We need a doctor! Is there a doctor in the court?"

People began to stand up and look around in alarm. Two policemen bent over Egleton and quickly unbuttoned his shirt. From the back of the room, a large man with a shock of white hair walked briskly toward the dock. "Please let me pass. I am the doctor."

He made his way through the crowd around the dock and leaned over Egleton. After a brief moment, he called out, "Get an ambulance, quick!"

The ambulance arrived in a matter of minutes. Two orderlies in white hurried Egleton off on a stretcher.

But it was too late. At 3:30, Saint Thomas's Hospital issued a laconic bulletin: "Mr. Dennis Egleton succumbed to a cardiac attack in the ambulance on the way to the hospital. He was dead on arrival."

When he heard the news, Jeff felt a strange disquiet. Perhaps it was the expression of a trapped animal on Egleton's face as he collapsed in the dock. For the first time, the mask of cool cynicism had fallen off. All that was left was a poor frightened soul, caught in a noose he couldn't loosen. Perhaps, after all, death was the least painful solution to Egleton's impasse.

It may have been this moment of truth — and some considerable curiosity — that led Jeff Saunders to attend Dennis Egleton's funeral. The man had no wife, no children. Nor had any of his colleagues at British Chemicals taken the trouble to attend. So on the morning of June 7, under a leaden sky, Jeff found himself in a small group of reporters and curiosity seekers as Dennis Harold Egleton was laid to rest in the cheerless cemetery at Lewes, Sussex.

From a small florist's shop near the cemetery, Jeff bought a bunch of flowers which he placed on the damp earth. They were chrysanthemums.

Part Two

A Year Later in Port-au-Prince

4

"CHRYSANTHEMUMS," Sullivan repeated.

The C.I.A. chief's eyes were riveted on the closed dossier in front of him. Then he looked up at Jeff Saunders who was busily lighting a cigar.

"It's been over a year since you attended Dennis Egleton's funeral in Sussex. You placed flowers on his grave. And here, more than a year after his death, Egleton is assassinated in Port-au-Prince in Haiti, and sorcerers burn his body in a voodoo ceremony. But they take the trouble to leave us a remnant: Egleton's right hand. To make certain that we can identify him through his fingerprints. So that we don't assume that the murdered man was just any victim of a casual murder. So that we know for sure that he is a man who died twice. I wonder what they have in store for us next . . ."

Jeff was silent. He had difficulty hiding his agitation. The events of that affair were all too clear in his mind: the scandal surrounding Crichton-Sloane, Brian Auchinleck's evasive explanations, the trial at the Old Bailey and, above all, the terror on Dennis Egleton's face as he collapsed in the dock. Could it all have been staged? He was ready to swear it wasn't. But the facts were there, insistent, irrefutable. The incinerated corpse may not have been identifiable. But the corpse had one hand. And that hand belonged to Dennis Egleton.

"This kind of thing just doesn't happen, Jeff," Sullivan said moodily.

Jeff still said nothing.

Sullivan got to his feet and stood by the large bay window. He parted the curtains and looked out at the night creeping over Washington. "People don't die twice," he went on, as if talking to himself. "They don't come back to life. And they don't get themselves slaughtered during a voodoo ceremony. Certainly not in Haiti today. I know the Haitians. They wouldn't do it."

Jeff had managed to shrug off the old memories and was trying to sort out the pieces of the puzzle. "You've read the dossier, Jim. But you haven't told me your conclusions. So far, I'm sure of only one thing: we were not supposed to know about Egleton's death. The general public wasn't supposed to know. Only one man: that priest, the undercover agent for the British. There's been a murder. I have no idea who committed it, but I'm dead certain it was no ritual murder. It was passed off as a ritual murder for the benefit of whoever discovered the body. The killers knew how terrified the Haitians are of voodoo. It was a kind of macabre joke, or more likely a confidential message aimed at the chief of M.I.6. A way of saying, 'We killed the man; nobody will know who he is, but just for your benefit, we've left his I.D. card — his fingerprints. You will undoubtedly recognize them. But the secret will remain between the two of us.' "

Sullivan continued looking out the window.

"As luck would have it, the British agent wasn't home.

The murder was exposed. But I'm sure the Haitian authorities couldn't have had Egleton's fingerprints." Sullivan turned to Saunders. "But we do. We have them. Joke or not, I can't simply close the case like that. And dismiss the fact that a master spy who died in England died a second time in Haiti."

"But there's something else too, isn't there, Jim," Saunders asked in a bantering tone.

Sullivan pounded the table with his fists. "You're damn right there is. You remember *why* we sent you to London last year?"

"The 'Crown Project'?"

"Precisely. And you know it was finally approved. The missile installations in Britain are already under way, and the first Goliaths will be shipped in the next few months. The operation is top-secret and the White House must be absolutely certain that there are no leaks."

"But you know that Auchinleck . . ."

"Sure, sure, Brian Auchinleck did a brilliant job of cleaning out the spies swarming all over England. But we have to be absolutely certain. The Goliath is important, Jeff. If the Russians succeed in getting their hands on the operational systems, they'll find a way to neutralize them in no time. That's why this charred corpse in Haiti makes me so damn nervous."

"You want me to clear the whole thing up, right, Jim?" Jeff said with the trace of a smile.

Sullivan nodded.

Jeff leaned over his boss's desk and pressed the intercom button. "May I?" He looked up at Sullivan who shrugged his shoulders. Talking rapidly into the apparatus, Saunders said, "Mary, be a good girl and get me the flight schedule for London."

"You're getting to be well known over there, Jeff," Sullivan observed. "I suppose this time you won't be needing your old friend Auchinleck?"

"Yes, I feel badly about that. But he deserves it." Jeff pressed the intercom button again. "Another thing, Mary. Ask Section D to prepare me a passport right away. They have a batch of my photographs, and at my age I'm not going in for disguises. Tell them to make me a Canadian passport. French Canadian. They can figure out a name. I'll need it tonight."

Turning to Sullivan, he said: "I speak French, and since Canada is part of the Commonwealth, I won't have any trouble at passport control."

And he was right. Less than a half hour after his BOAC Jumbo Jet landed on Heathrow's rain-slicked tarmac, Raymond Lechartier, a tourist from Quebec, walked through the glass doors of Terminal Number 2 and headed for the Hertz counter. As he signed the form, he blessed the C.I.A. counterfeiters who had not only prepared him a splendid passport, but also a whole array of documents, including a driver's license and a letter of credit to Barclay's Bank. With a twinge of regret, he passed over the E-type Jaguar which the girl at the counter suggested after looking him over with an experienced eye. No, a Jaguar would be too noticeable, especially in a small village. So he made do with a black Ford Cortina.

He drove cautiously. After leaving London, he crossed Surrey and headed for Sussex, consulting from time to time the road map he found in the glove compartment. He ate a tasteless lunch at Burgess Hill, and decided on further thought that he would do well to spend the night there. For lack of anything better, he took one of the five rooms in a pub called the Red Lion. He spent the afternoon in his room, and when evening came, had a frugal supper sent up.

Outside, the rain was falling in buckets, but in any case, it seemed wiser not to show himself in public. To be sure, this wasn't really an operational mission, but it wasn't a publicity stunt either. His dinner eaten, he placed the tray outside his door and turned off the light. Snatches of conversation, a few bars of a song, bursts of drunken laughter reached him from the pub. The rain continued to beat against his window. He fell asleep.

The insistent buzz of the tiny alarm in his wristwatch woke him at exactly midnight. He listened: the rain was still drumming at his window, but not a sound came from below. The house was absolutely silent. He dressed quickly in warm dark-colored clothes. Hesitating briefly, he left his raincoat in the closet. Where he was heading, its light color would stand out too clearly. He would be soaked to the skin, but there was nothing for it. He tiptoed down the stairs, walked silently to the Cortina, started the motor and switched on the windshield wipers.

The road was deserted. Actually, the torrential rain was a blessing: it kept other cars off the road and made undesirable encounters unlikely. Jeff confidently took one narrow road, then another. He had learned the way by heart during the afternoon spent in his room. After a half hour's drive, he arrived at his destination and parked the car near an iron gate in a low wall. He opened the trunk and took out a shovel he had bought that morning in Sevenoaks. He leaped over the gate and looked carefully around him. This was the place where he had been over a year ago: the cemetery in Lewes.

He advanced slowly through the tall grass, a silent silhouette moving wraithlike from one grave to the next, leaning over the headstones and training his flashlight on the inscriptions. The icy rain rolled down his face and neck; his clothes were soon drenched and he shook with the cold.

There were claps of thunder in the distance and an occasional pale shaft of lightning lit up the monuments. His feet became tangled in the wet grass and sank in the mud around the graves. From time to time, he stopped to look around. Yes, he was alone in the desolate place, alone on this dismal night, sneaking like a thief from one grave to another, from one name to another.

He finally found Dennis Egleton's grave under an isolated willow. Turning his flashlight on for a split second, he read the inscription on the stone:

DENNIS HAROLD EGLETON
REQUIESCAT IN PACE

He had no time to waste. With a burst of energy, he aimed his shovel at the mound next to the stone and started digging. He worked with a frenzy, as if possessed, faster and faster. The blood throbbed in his temples and his breathing came in painful gasps. He stopped only to wipe his face with his wet sleeve. Alert to every sound, to the thunder coming closer, the gusts of wind in the trees, the thousand tiny night sounds, he found himself casting nervous glances behind him. The rain was running down the sides of the hole in little rivulets and turning the earth into a quagmire which clung to his shovel and made digging increasingly difficult.

Finally he heard the sound of wood. The shovel had struck the coffin. Redoubling his efforts, he swung away at the rest of the earth in the hole, hurling it to the side. Slowly, the black coffin lid emerged, lit by an occasional flash of lightning. Jeff crouched and, using a chisel, pried open the lid.

In the fraction of a second during which his frozen hands lifted the lid and a bolt of lightning illumined the interior, he felt a sharp pain explode in his neck. With a rasping groan, he fell unconscious by the open grave of Dennis Harold Egleton.

The pain throbbed through his body, like something alive and insidious which had crept inside and was hammering with methodical obstinacy. It gripped his neck, attacked his skull. His forehead and temples were dripping sweat. There was a bitter, slimy taste in his mouth. He tried to turn his head but the pain made him bite his lips to keep from crying out. The years of training had taught him not to show pain. It was this same training that now told him not to open his eyes wide or try to sit up. Instead he slowly started to flutter his eyelids, stealing quick glances at the scene around him. Gradually he pieced it together: he was in a small room with a high ceiling and a wooden table surrounded by three chairs. To the right was a tall window framed with heavy draperies. It didn't seem to be barred which meant a possible avenue of escape. As if turning in his sleep, he now concentrated his fluttering gaze on the left side of the room. Out of the corner of his eye he could just see a door. Then he saw something else: a man of imposing build sitting next to the door in his shirt-sleeves. He was holding a newspaper, and the handle of a revolver protruded from the holster strapped under his left armpit.

Jeff was stretched out on an old iron cot and covered with a rough wool blanket. His wet and muddy clothes lay on the floor next to the bed, and he could see that the seams in his jacket were ripped. There were scattered odds and ends on the table, probably the contents of his pockets. Some shiny silver and a white handkerchief caught his eye. They must have gone through his things with a fine-tooth comb.

He turned his face to the wall and as his swollen neck rubbed against the coarse mattress he let out a cry of pain. He heard the guard leap to his feet, a door squeak and the sound of whispering. Someone rushed up to the bed and leaned over him. A deep full voice asked him, "So, Mr. Lechartier, how are we feeling this morning?"

Jeff managed to raise himself on his elbows and turned his head. The man he saw was about forty, of medium height, wearing a black turtleneck sweater under a gray suit. He seemed fairly undistinguished except for an intelligent gleam in his small brown eyes and an even cultivated voice.

Jeff looked at him without speaking.

"So, what's new in Canada?" the man continued. "You are a very active Canadian. Barely off the plane, you rent a car, head for the south and go out in the dead of night to commune with nature. We don't see that kind of tourist much anymore." His bantering tone changed abruptly and became menacing. "What are you looking for, Mr. Lechartier or whoever you are?"

"And who are you?" Jeff asked calmly. He had the clear impression that these were not members of the police.

"I will ask the questions," the voice said icily. "Who sent you here?"

Jeff said nothing.

"George! Tony!"

The man with the revolver and a younger ruddy-faced man rushed into the room and closed the door behind them. The unidentified man in the gray suit leaned over Jeff. "Let's get to the point. You are, I think, a professional. We examined you thoroughly. You have several scars on your body that could come only from small-arms fire. The condition of your muscles indicates that you are in top physical shape. You carefully hid the key to your room at the Red Lion in your car before you went off to play your archaeological games in the cemetery. It took us hell's own time to find it. The only things you had on you were obviously false papers. You went to work immediately on your arrival. Which can only mean that it had all been planned in advance."

He paused for a moment. "So much for you. Now, for what concerns us: those two boys and I aren't amateurs either. George" — he indicated the taller of the two — "is the one who hit you last night. He could just as easily have reduced you to permanent silence. It wouldn't have been the first time.

"I'm sure you've already noticed the window and thought of escaping that way. Put it out of your mind. I have two men downstairs and a third at the door. And remember this: nobody knows you're here. An nobody is going to know. We can do anything with you we like. So I advise you to start talking. If you don't, George and Tony will give you a demonstration of their skills that will make you curse the day you were born."

"Do as you please," Jeff replied coldly.

"So you're not going to tell us anything?" The man straightened up and looked at him thoughtfully. "I suppose you really won't." He raised his arms in mock helplessness. "If we're not going to get anything out of you, you leave us no choice. We'll wait a little, then we'll kill you. It's that simple. You won't get out of here alive."

Jeff looked at him with indifference.

"You don't believe me?"

"Enough of that, Burton. Stop the nonsense." Another voice, this one all too familiar, came from the direction of the door. "He knows as well as you do that we don't kill people that way."

Jeff turned his head in surprise. In the doorway stood Sir Brian Auchinleck.

*

A pale autumn sun reddened the low clouds rolling in from the east. Then it began its descent behind the Hampshire hills.

"I must admit I had no idea they were your men," Saunders said to Sir Brian.

The American agent and the head of British counterintelligence were sitting comfortably on the back seat of the black Bentley as it hummed its way back to London. Sir Brian leaned forward and pressed a button. The glass partition between them and the chauffeur slowly rose.

"I thought they were working for the Russians," Saunders went on. He wore a bandage around his neck and the dark circles under his eyes indicated his fatigue. His clothes still carried traces of sticky mud.

Auchinleck didn't answer. He looked straight ahead, then he turned to Jeff, his face red with anger.

"I should have thrown you out of the country."

"Oh really?" Jeff said.

"You come in under a false identity, with a fake passport, and you behave as if you were in enemy territory. For the first time in twenty-two years, I catch an American agent sneaking into England and carrying on as if he were in Russia or China. You should be thrown out for this."

"But I won't be, will I, Brian?"

"And why not?" Auchinleck snapped. "Would you be good enough to tell me . . ."

"Oh, come on. Let's stop this stupid game." Then, looking Sir Brian straight in the eyes and measuring every word, he said, "You know as well as I do that that damn coffin was empty."

Sir Brian sat quietly for a moment. Then he muttered:

"Burton and his men weren't as efficient as I'd hoped . . ."

"No, they weren't," Jeff agreed. "They were about two seconds late. They got to me just after I had opened the coffin. That coffin was empty, Brian, and you knew it all along."

Auchinleck continued to stare out the window. "I had counted on them," he went on. "First-class men. Burton is a veteran of my operational services. So are his men. They were handpicked. Their orders were to make absolutely certain no one got near that grave." He was silent for a moment, then added, "I suppose it wasn't that simple, really. They couldn't just stand there by the grave all day and all night. They had to be discreet. Oh, damn, *damn*. What a bloody stupid mistake!"

He turned and fixed his eyes on Jeff. "I've got to know who's in on this besides you. I suppose Jim Sullivan? And how did you get this far? You've got to tell me. This case is much more serious than you think." His voice had regained a little of its usual assurance.

"I have nothing to hide, which is more than some people can say," Jeff replied. "In any case, you'll know the details sooner or later, and as for the rest of it you'll probably guess it all without my help. You remember that over a year ago I sat in on Egleton's trial. I also went to his funeral. A week ago, his incinerated body was found in Haiti. The people who killed him tried to let your man know . . . that priest of yours."

"Finchley," Sir Brian said with impatience. "Finchley. He's not one of my men. He's with M.I.6."

"I know he is," Jeff said. "Anyway, he wasn't home. And, as you know, the story got out. One of our men took the victim's fingerprints and sent them to us. We ran them through our computer index. When the report came back, Jim was astounded. So was I, of course. It was perfectly natural that he send me to find out if in fact Egleton was dead and buried in Lewes. I don't think more than three men in the agency are in on it. Sullivan may have told the President. At the time, the President was very much concerned, as you know. Because of Crichton-Sloane."

"But why didn't you get in touch with me?" Sir Brian said reproachfully.

"Now, come on, please." Jeff's patience was wearing thin. "At the time of the trial, you were as slippery as an eel. Of course, I didn't understand why. I thought perhaps you didn't want me to know too much about your methods. But when we uncovered the business about the fingerprints, we began to get the picture. Sullivan and I realized you knew the whole story all along. You knew that Egleton was neither dead nor buried. I suppose you were even the stage director for his death scene. We're not so stupid as to imagine that British intelligence would let a master spy pretend he was dead and escape somewhere, while an inspired accomplice exchanged bodies at the hospital and sent you a fake for the funeral. That only happens in third-rate thrillers."

"Correct," Sir Brian said crisply. "And what are your conclusions?"

"My conclusions? I don't know everything, to be sure. But it seems obvious that this Finchley alerted you as soon as he returned to Port-au-Prince and found out about the burned corpse on the Colline des Esprits. And then you immediately sent a crew down to Lewes to prevent anyone's getting at the grave. You knew that before your man could get back to Port-au-Prince, someone else might get to the fingerprints and identify Egleton.

"To tell you the truth," Jeff continued, "even if I hadn't opened the lid of that coffin, I would have known that Egleton hadn't died of a heart attack at the Old Bailey. Just the fact that you were having the grave guarded was evidence enough."

"And what do you plan to do now?"

"Now? Well, right now, Brian, I am waiting for you to tell me the entire story down to the last detail. What does it all mean? Why the elaborate production? Why the heart attack and the burial of the empty coffin? What was Egleton doing in Haiti and who, in your opinion, murdered him? You have to tell me, Brian. And if it's convincing enough, maybe Jim Sullivan will agree to stop right here. But only on condition that we learn everything. Until we do, I don't budge."

Sir Brian looked at him without speaking.

"You have no choice," Jeff said. "What else can you do? Washington knows why I'm here. You can't shut me up or make me forget what I saw. And as you yourself said to your bully-boy Burton, I know as well as you do that you don't kill people that way."

Lancaster Gate was deserted. The night was clear but a cold wind swept through the street in sudden gusts. Somewhere a clock struck ten. Jeff crossed the small garden and knocked on the service door. It opened immediately, as if the old servant looking him over coldly had been waiting for him behind it.

"Good evening, sir," he said in a neutral tone. "The gentlemen are expecting you in the library. Follow me, if you will."

They walked together down a long corridor which opened into a spacious hall with a spiral staircase leading to the floor above. The servant knocked on a heavy oak door at the far end of the room and, as he pushed it open, announced,

"The gentleman you are expecting is here, sir."

"Thank you, Miles," said a clipped voice. Jeff found himself in a vast library. The walls were covered with books from floor to ceiling. A large desk on which various papers, notebooks and pens were impeccably arranged stood in one corner, and, behind it, a high-backed wooden chair. Several deep leather armchairs were grouped around a large fireplace in which a fire burned brightly. It was the workroom of a soldier: large, orderly, unpretentious.

Two men were sitting in the chairs by the hearth. One of them was Sir Brian Auchinleck. The other one Jeff knew by sight although they had never met. He was General James Fleming, chief of M.I.6, a paunchy sixty-year-old with a thick mustache and intelligent eyes.

"I'm glad to meet you, Mr. Saunders," he said with little enthusiasm. "I've known your chief, Jim Sullivan, for a long time. I had him on the phone not an hour ago — at Sir Brian's suggestion — and he assured me that I could speak to you quite openly. I suppose you're asking yourself why Sir Brian wanted this interview. I will tell you that in a moment. But first let me add that before I agreed to this meeting, I received the assent of our Under-Secretary of State for Foreign Affairs who, as you know, presides over our Secret Intelligence Services. And the Under-Secretary in turn received the green light from the Prime Minister, the Foreign Secretary and the Home Secretary."

Jeff was duly impressed and gave the general a small deferential bow. Then he sat down in the armchair offered him and happily accepted a glass of brandy.

James Fleming took a brown dossier from his desk and started leafing through it. "I'd like to read you a résumé of some of the information on the Russian bloc we've compiled over the past twenty years." The pride in the general's voice was undisguised as he added, "If I may be so bold, I would say that this intelligence represents one of our services' more remarkable achievements.   For obvious reasons, I cannot show you the original documents."

Jeff nodded and took a sip of brandy. He couldn't for the life of him see the connection between his mission and the comportment of his host, but he said nothing.

James Fleming began to read from the dossier:

" 'July 10, 1955: A secret accord for the sale of a large quantity of armaments has been concluded between the Soviet Union and Egypt. The Russians are to furnish Egypt one hundred and forty jet fighters, two hundred "Stalin" and T-54 tanks two hundred half-tracks and seven submarines.' This accord was not made public until September 17, 1955, when Sir Humphrey Trevelyan, our ambassador in Cairo, made representations to President Nasser."

General Fleming took a deep breath and continued: " 'November 3, 1955. Serious differences have erupted between China and the Soviet Union. Relations between the Kremlin and Chairman Mao Tse-tung have reached crisis proportions.' " Fleming stopped and eyed Saunders. "I don't know if you are fully aware of the importance of that event. It was the first information on the Soviet-Chinese split to reach the West.

" 'February 26, 1956: In a confidential statement to the Twentieth Congress of the Soviet Communist Party, the Secretary-General, Nikita Khrushchev, denounced "the atrocities and barbarous crimes committed by Stalin." ' "

Fleming again interrupted his reading: "The complete text of Khrushchev's speech is attached to this report. The other intelligence services didn't receive it until four months later.

" 'October 21, 1956: Intervention by the Russian Army in

Hungary to crush the rebellion in Budapest appears to be imminent. However, military intervention in Poland is not expected.'

" 'May 1, 1960: Nikita Khrushchev decides to sabotage the summit conference of the four major powers in Paris as a result of the American U-2 shot down over Russia.

" 'October 15, 1962: The Soviet Union decides not to risk military confrontation with the United States after its discovery of missile bases secretly installed by Russia in Cuba.

" 'August 18, 1968: An invasion of Czechoslovakia by the Red Army is expected at any moment to overturn the liberal regime of Alexander Dubček.

" 'June 12, 1970.' " The chief of M.I.6 looked up from his papers: "The next report is a detailed study of the Soviet ICBM network and the stock of nuclear bombs in the U.S.S.R. That's all I can tell you. It's top-secret.

" 'November 5, 1972: Tomorrow the Soviet Union will suspend delivery of military equipment to North Vietnam to compel her to sign a peace treaty with the United States.'

"I also have here some photographs I'd like you to look at." One by one, he handed Saunders a series of enlargements.

"The military port of Odessa in 1969."

Jeff examined the photograph which was stamped "Top-secret."

"This one is of a line of fortifications on the Chinese-Russian border, taken the same year."

Fleming handed Jeff another photograph. "These twenty-odd generals and civilians are the men responsible for the Russian missile program. We have been able to identify almost all of them. The picture was taken in 1971. Here's another from 1972, showing the most sophisticated Soviet missile, the S.S.-74. The existence of this missile is still a secret. We've told only the United States about it."

Fleming retrieved the photographs. "As you can see, I've quoted only a small part of the information in this dossier," he said, tapping the thick folder with his finger. "Almost all the material here is top-secret. Its value cannot be overestimated."

Jeff cleared his throat. "I'm well aware of that, sir, and believe me, I appreciate . . . but I don't understand . . ."

"You don't understand the connection with your presence here tonight." Fleming gave a curious smile. "You see, Mr. Saunders, all this information, all these photographs — plus hundreds of others — have a common denominator. They all came from the same source. From one of our agents whom we called Satellite-2. He was perhaps the greatest spy of the twentieth century. In any case, he was the best agent we had in the Soviet Union and in our service during the past twenty years. He took enormous risks; he was ready to sacrifice his life for England."

Fleming paused and looked hard at Jeff. "Satellite-2's real name was Dennis Harold Egleton."

5

"EGLETON!" Jeff put down his glass and looked from Jame
Fleming to Brian Auchinleck in stunned disbelief. The
gazed back at him with solemn impassive faces.

"I find this hard to believe," he said after a moment. "Eg
leton one of your agents? It doesn't seem —"

"James hasn't told you all," Auchinleck broke in. "Egleto
was no ordinary spy. He was an extraordinary doub
agent. For over twenty years, this man fed the Russian
false information on England's military installations and he
strategic power. To make absolutely sure they trusted him
we even sacrificed several secrets of prime importance
They had complete faith in him. They were convinced tha
Dennis Egleton was a dedicated Communist who would d
anything for them. To this day, most of their reports, analy
ses and evaluations concerning England are based on infor
mation conceived at M.I.6 headquarters and faithfully trans
mitted by Egleton. As their trusted ally, he took courses i
the most secret institutions of Russian espionage. He ha
access to the top officials of the K.G.B. He had woven a we
of relationships in Moscow that permitted him to receive in

ormation of the greatest value. He had become the prin-
ipal adviser on British affairs to their psychological warfare
division; he was also in charge of filtering and evaluating
much of the material coming from other sources."

"Just a minute," Saunders said. "There's something I
don't understand. If all that you say is true, why the hell did
you bring him to trial?"

Fleming took up the story. "Perhaps we ought to go back
a little. Don't forget that we spent several years preparing
Egleton for this mission. He learned Russian, he studied
Russian culture, then he devised a foolproof cover as a businessman. By 1953, he was the head of an electronics company that even supplied our own navy. Posing as a left-wing
idealist, he made contact with the Russians and offered them
information. In 1965, when he had been completely accepted by them, we had him named representative of British
Chemicals in Moscow. We kept our contact with him
through our commercial mission in the Moscow embassy
which carried out the exchange of telegrams between him
and his firm in London. Things were going splendidly until
the wretched Crichton-Sloane affair."

"Ah, Crichton-Sloane!" Jeff said, as he began to see daylight. "It's about time you told me the truth about that business."

"You may be surprised to learn that Egleton's deposition
at the trial conformed almost to the letter with the actual
truth. The Russians were very annoyed indeed about the
dismantling of their network in England. And they really
did try at the last moment to bring down their sworn enemy,
Stanley Crichton-Sloane, in the general debacle. On the 14th
of May, just as Egleton said at the hearing, they had him
compose several texts to incriminate Crichton-Sloane.
Among them was the letter to Manoli Theodoris, and the

M.P.'s handwriting was counterfeited in their laboratories
Up to that point, everything dovetails. What followed, how
ever, is quite different."

"But why didn't he tell you immediately what he'd done?"

General Fleming gave him a patronizing smile. "My dea
Mr. Saunders, you must be sufficiently familiar with thi
kind of work to realize that one cannot always telephone or
send a telegram when one wants to. Egleton had to be ex
tremely careful, precisely because he was involved in a top
secret K.G.B. maneuver. He knew that telegrams and tele
phone calls from the British commercial mission would be
under particularly close surveillance. He had to take specia
precautions. Besides, he didn't think that the affair was al
that pressing. He had no way of knowing that a K.G.B. em
issary would be leaving for London with the fake letter al
most immediately."

"In that case, how did you get him to go to Geneva?"

Fleming laughed. "We didn't. He went all by himself."

Saunder's eyebrows shot up.

"Look: Manoli Theodoris was murdered on May 16. On
the 17th, the news had spread over the entire planet. But i
wasn't until late afternoon on the 18th that *France-Soir*
printed the reproduction of the letter attributed to Crichton-
Sloane. Moscow didn't learn of it until the 19th. Egleton
was completely dumbfounded. Suddenly, here he was the
unwitting accomplice of a diabolical plot to demolish the
private life and political career of an innocent man. He
knew that only he could clear Crichton-Sloane. He understood public opinion all too well. Even if the case against
Crichton-Sloane were dismissed, the British would continue
to suspect him and his future would be seriously compro-
mised. Therefore the only way to save his reputation was to
make a clean breast of it before a tribunal.

"So, at his request, we sent him a telegram, as if from British Chemicals Limited, asking him to come to Geneva right away. He took the plane for Geneva, but left the very same day for London. That was May 20th. He arrived here at my place at midnight and told me the whole story. I then called Brian and asked him to come over."

Sir Brian picked up the thread. "We stayed with him in this very room until seven in the morning. After discussing the pros and cons, we all came to the same conclusion: the only way to clear Crichton-Sloane was to have Egleton publicly expose the plot. In order to do that, we had to arrest him as a Soviet spy and bring him to trial. Obviously this also meant that his clandestine activities would come to an end, but we had no choice. The essential thing was to keep the Russians from suspecting anything. They had to continue to believe that Egleton was their man and that we had unmasked him. Otherwise, had they learned his real role, had they suspected for a minute that he might be one of our own agents, his twenty years' patient labor would have been wasted. So, we had to find an excuse to arrest him, bring him to trial and punish him in such a way that the Russians would continue to believe in the authenticity of the false information he had furnished them.

"Egleton informed us that it was Kolodni, his contact in Moscow, who had gone to London and given the letter to Sheila MacAlister. So we thought up the following: our counterespionage service would discover that Kolodni had met with Sheila a few hours before she took the plane for France. We would discover at the same time that he had a very close relationship with the representative of British Chemicals in Moscow — Dennis Egleton. We would have suspected for some time that Egleton might be working for the Russians. Using a business meeting in Geneva as a pretext, we got him to Geneva, then to London in order to interrogate him. It would be during this interrogation that he'd get bogged down in contradictions and lies and end up telling all."

"An inspired plot," Saunders remarked.

"Yes, but we also had to convince our government," Sir Brian chuckled. "That wasn't so easy. Here we are, dreaming up a plot that thumbs its nose at British justice, and all of it merely to save a Member of Parliament — and of the Opposition too, remember — from having his name sullied."

"Yes, I see," Jeff said. At least, he now understood why Sir Brian had seemed so nervous when he saw an American agent arrive to attend the trial. Auchinleck had worried that an old fox like him might smell a rat and find the shuttling between Moscow, Geneva and London a little odd, not to mention the fact that the Egleton who had dropped from the skies as if by chance was the same man who had composed the incriminating letter.

"I must admit that your Egleton was an exceptionally gifted actor. He had me completely convinced during the trial. What I don't understand is why he had to have that heart attack."

"I don't know how well you are acquainted with our system of justice," Sir Brian said. "A British court is not something to be trifled with, much less made an accessory to a crime. The trial had to be absolutely authentic. We chose the 'heart attack' as the best way to get him off the stage before the verdict."

"And from the hospital straight to Haiti?" Saunders said half mockingly.

"He never reached the hospital. Before the last day's session, he was given an injection to make him lose consciousness with all the symptoms of heart failure. As for Haiti, we had worked that out with him in advance. We couldn't send him to jail, then simulate an escape. It was clear that so long as he was alive, the Russians would be on his trail to avenge his betrayal. So we passed him off for dead, gave him a new identity and shipped him off where no one was likely to find him. He chose Haiti himself. Tourists are few and far between, and, so far as we knew, the Russians didn't operate there. We decided that after a few years in Haiti, when everything had calmed down again, he could establish a new identity in Australia or New Zealand. Naturally he could never come back to England."

"What identity did you give him?"

"We made him an Australian, with a passport in the name of Roderick Brandon. He passed himself off as an amateur painter who had decided to spend a few years in Haiti studying the native art. Before he left, he let his beard grow and picked up some Bohemian ways along with a little knowledge about art. He left for Port-au-Prince about a year ago. Our agent in Haiti knew about him but had no notion of his real identity."

Jeff looked up. "But they found him anyway."

Sir Brian studied the dying embers in the fireplace. "Yes," he said, "they found him."

The taxi maneuvered through the evening rush hour and stopped before the Houses of Parliament. Jeff scanned the old towers which to so many symbolized Britain, and entered the long gallery flanked by marble busts and time-scarred portraits of kings and lords. At the entrance to the large vaulted waiting room, he stopped to fill out the traditional green form, and glanced distractedly at the emblems on the walls, the massive chandelier, and the Lords and Members talking to their deferential visitors. He handed the form to one of the ushers and examined the crowd of people waiting patiently on the benches along the walls for the Member they had asked to see.

He heard a discreet cough behind him. An usher in tails with stiff collar and white bow tie addressed him: "Mr. Saunders, will you come this way?" He followed him along a labyrinth of dark halls, stairways and deserted passages. As they started to climb a spiral staircase, he realized they must be in one of the towers. The usher led him through a small shabby office where a bespectacled secretary was working, and knocked on a black door, flattening himself against the wall to let Saunders pass.

From his desk next to a narrow gothic window, a tall elegant man rose to his feet and came forward with outstretched hand. Seen up close, the familiar face which a year before had been spread across the front pages of the world was even more impressive. His smile was open and his clasp firm and friendly.

"Very good of you to come," he said.

Stanley Crichton-Sloane offered Jeff an armchair which had seen better days. Jeff's glance took in the room. It was low-ceilinged and in need of a coat of paint. A pale light filtered through the narrow window. Crichton-Sloane had followed his gaze. Smiling, he said, "Yes, I know. It's hardly like your senators' offices in Washington. But I'm considered one of the lucky ones to have an office here instead of across the street."

He examined Saunders with undisguised curiosity.

"So you are the man who is in on one of the best-kept secrets in the kingdom. Has Fleming told you that most of the members in the present government — not to mention the preceding one — know less than you do? At the time, the Egleton affair was resolved within the cabinet. After our

ictory in the last elections, only the most important
nembers in the new government were let in on the secret.
When Fleming told me why you were here, I asked him to
et up this meeting. As you know, I too have a small stake in
he secret."

"Were you in on it from the beginning?"

"No, I wasn't." Crichton-Sloane lit his pipe and leaned
orward. "I knew nothing more than what was in the pa-
ers. It was only when the new government was formed
fter the elections that I was invited to meet the chiefs of the
wo services. That's when I learned that Egleton wasn't
lead, that he was in fact a double agent. Then last week, Sir
Brian Auchinleck came to tell me that Egleton had been as-
assinated in Haiti, apparently by the Russians."

Saunders saw a look of distress in his eyes. The M.P. con-
inued: "I can't help feeling a certain degree of guilt. After
ll, the man died because of me. When he learned what was
oing on, he could have simply sent a report from Moscow.
But instead he chose to come here. That meant putting an
nd to his activities, exposing himself — all in order to save
ne." He paused and examined his hands. "Then the Rus-
ians found him."

Grasping his desk and looking straight at Jeff, he said,
But I promise you I will find a way to avenge him in turn.
must know who did it. The Russians couldn't have picked
ip his traces all by themselves."

Jeff nodded. Crichton-Sloane went on: "Somebody here,
omebody inside our Security Services, must have informed
hem, and I'm going to do everything in my power to help
xpose that traitor."

Jeff was impressed by Crichton-Sloane's sincerity, but he
ad come for something else.

"Are you certain that he saved you?"

"No doubt about it. Without his deposition at the trial,
would never have been able to make it back — even if th
government had never brought me to trial. After his testi
mony I regained my party's complete confidence; I was onc
again in the public's good graces. Did you know that I wa
elected with almost twice the number of votes this time? N
candidate from my party has ever had such a victory. Mos
gratifying." He added with a smile, "You know, we Britis
are always on the side of the underdog — of the person wh
has suffered an injustice. That was a big thing in my favor.'

"But you didn't get the portfolio you were supposed to
did you?" Jeff said carefully. "You were a member of th
shadow cabinet, and now —"

Crichton-Sloane interrupted him. "Quite the contrary.
was I who refused to enter the cabinet in spite of th
prompting of my friends."

Saunders looked at him with surprise.

Crichton-Sloane rose to his feet and started pacing bac
and forth. "You must understand. I know myself only to
well. I know my assets and my limitations. As Sir Isaia
Berlin once said, 'A man is not truly free until he ha
learned to know his limitations.' I am very conscious of m
own. I always have been."

He was interrupted by a knock on the door. He waite
impatiently while his secretary entered with the tea tray an
placed it on a corner of his desk. On it were a brown teapo
two cups and saucers and some biscuits on a paper plate. A
soon as the door had closed behind her, he continued:

"I don't know how much you know about me. I com
from an extremely poor family. There were times when w
didn't have enough to eat. My father was from the middl
class, but he went bankrupt in the crisis of 1929 and die
soon after."

"I had no idea you were a self-made man," Jeff said.

"That surprises me. I thought the press was rather keen about the lowly beginnings of the glamorous M.P." Crichton-Sloane laughed and walked over to the tea tray. 'Forgive me, I am forgetting my manners. Would you care for some tea?"

"Yes, thank you," Saunders said, and Crichton-Sloane poured the dark brew into the two cups and sat down behind his desk.

"My mother brought up my brother and me in a slum in Newcastle. As a boy, I swore that I would get out of there, get an education and make something of myself."

His eyes focusing on his teacup, he spoke in an intense monotone. "I worked at night, Sundays, holidays. I worked myself to the bone to pay my way through school. I tried every trade: miner, washer-up, delivery boy, newsboy, shoeshine boy. Then came the day" — he looked at Saunders with a gleam of pride in his eyes — "that I was admitted to Trinity College, Cambridge, along with the sons of the rich, the elite of Britain. And I did better than any of them. I showed them what I was capable of. I even said at the time" — he let out a self-deprecating laugh — "that one day I would be Great Britain's Foreign Secretary. I studied like a man possessed: international relations, diplomacy, finance, foreign languages. And in all modesty I believe that today I am my party's undisputed leader in these fields."

He saw Jeff's glance take in a photograph on his desk. He smiled. "Yes, my wife. She is rich, she comes from an aristocratic family, but I think I can say in all fairness that I didn't need either her money or her title. I was already launched. After trying my hand at diplomacy, first as a diplomatic correspondent for several newspapers, then in the Foreign Office, I stood for Parliament. I was first elected twelve years ago, but foreign affairs continued to be my main interest. I began to speak out openly against the Russians. They would have loved to shut me up but, as you know, they didn't succeed. And I was given the European Affairs portfolio."

"But you say that you didn't want that post in the present government?" Jeff asked in some bewilderment.

"No, I didn't. So long as England was not in the Common Market, so long as she had to fight to get in, so long as she had to convince, charm, threaten — I wanted it. But from the moment she was admitted, it became a job for an expert on the price of eggs and ball bearings."

"What is it you want then?" Jeff tried not to sound too insistent. From below came the sad hoot of a barge as it made its way up the Thames. Crichton-Sloane glanced toward the window.

"I wanted Foreign Affairs. But it had already been promised to someone who had seniority over me. I decided to wait. I am now chairman of the committee on Foreign Affairs in the Commons . . . and I wait."

"You wait for what?" Jeff kept trying for a chink in the armor.

Crichton-Sloane lowered his voice slightly. "Our Foreign Secretary — Anthony Ashcroft — is no longer young. Two years ago, before we came into power, he had a serious heart attack. He already had the post in the shadow cabinet. After the election he announced to a closed meeting of party leaders that he had no intention of dying at his post. So we entered into a gentleman's agreement that I would succeed him when he retired — within the year, he said. Well, a year has passed . . ." Crichton-Sloane shrugged his shoulders, "and I'm still waiting."

Jeff took a box of cigars from his pocket. "May I?" he

sked, since Crichton-Sloane seemed in no hurry to be rid of
is visitor. He lit one and said,

"Would it be indiscreet of me to ask what your goals will
e once you are Foreign Minister?"

"Obviously, I will be primarily concerned with seeing that
ngland continues to play an important role in the world —
nd an independent one, not tied to the apron strings of the
nited States. And of course I have certain personal goals.
s Foreign Secretary, I will be responsible for the Security
ervices. In that capacity, I intend to do everything in my
ower to get to the bottom of Egleton's murder. I'm going
shake M.I.6 like a fig tree until I find the traitor who de-
vered Egleton to the Russians." He stopped abruptly with
1 apologetic laugh. "Look, I'm frightfully sorry. I've
lked your ear off. Now tell me, what are *your* plans?"

"My plans? Oh, I think my work in England is finished.
ve already informed Washington of the results. I'll go to
aiti now and try to complete our investigation. Then back
Washington. I assume the English will keep after the
gleton business from this end." Jeff rose to his feet.

"I know we will." Crichton-Sloane rose too and looked
ff directly in the eyes. "But I rely on you. Since you are
ping to Haiti, I beg you to find out exactly what happened.
ou'll be doing me a personal favor. Let me know of any
idence, any clue that will help our own investigation. On
r side, I promise you all the help in our power. I know
u are one of the best agents in the C.I.A., Mr. Saunders,
d I'd be grateful if you could help me repay my debt to
ennis Egleton."

The two men shook hands warmly and Jeff left.

In the cold light of dawn, the plane rose through the fog
d headed out over the rough waters of the Channel. Jeff

closed his eyes. He was once again on the threshold of a dangerous mission. In six hours, he would be landing in New York, then on to Haiti and the mystery that lay behind an incinerated corpse.

6

STRANGE SOUNDS came from the distance.

The rays of the setting sun touched the verdant hills and tufted jungle that framed the bay, glittered for a moment on the crest of the dark waves and disappeared. Night fell suddenly, turning the mountains into looming shadows; the palms thrust waving fronds against the sky, the distant rolling of the waves became a muffled roar. Jeff was familiar with nights in the tropics, the stunning abruptness of their descent. At first he didn't recognize the low rumbling that began to emerge out of the dark shadows — a kind of smothered rhythmic beat that gradually grew in intensity, rising from the depths of the forests, descending from the tops of the hills, the summit of the mountains. Wave after wave, the sounds rolled in. They were the sounds of another universe, another world. The sound of tom-toms.

Then came the first fire, far off in the mountains above Kenscoff. Then another, then a third and many more, from the crests of the mountains and distant hills, from the heart of the jungle. Fires appeared everywhere, like lightning bugs dancing to the roll of the tom-toms.

Jeff turned to the trembling Haitian standing near him.

"What is that?" he asked.

The young black slowly turned his head toward him.

"Voodoo," he whispered, a flash of terror in his wide-open eyes. "Voodoo, sir."

Jeff probed the night, trying to break down the wall of distance and race, to understand the meaning of these secret ceremonies in which no white man had ever taken part. A mixture of smells wafted through the tropical night — the heady fragrance of exotic flowers, the odor of burning wood and incense, whiffs of rum and smoke. The wind brought distant sounds of song, of chants hammered out to the rhythm of the drums, the beating of feet and sudden piercing shrieks. Voodoo. Saturday night had fallen over Haiti, and throughout the island, on the hills, in forest clearings, far from prying strangers, thousands of blacks celebrated the cult of their cruel gods.

Sweating profusely, Jeff undid his tie and threw his jacket on the back seat of the car. He found it hard to adjust to this sudden and total metamorphosis. Only a few hours ago, he had arrived from New York, swaddled in his winter clothes, dreading the contest which would pit him against one of the world's craftiest adversaries. As he sat in Kennedy Airport, a courier from Washington had handed him a sealed envelope containing his papers. Everything was made out in his own name; he would have no use for a Canadian identity in Haiti. It also included a letter from Jim Sullivan giving him explicit instructions written out in the code they had devised before Jeff left for London. Because of the top-secret nature of his mission, reinforced by the concern of the British Secret Services, the C.I.A. chief had personally taken charge. Jeff gave the courier his Canadian papers and a report on his investigation in England which he had written on the plane in code. Then he boarded the plane for Haiti.

He spent most of the trip studying the documents which detailed various aspects of the operation, the methods of liaison and action to be used. He learned the addresses, passwords and his new *curriculum vitae* by heart. As the plane began its descent toward Haiti, Saunders slipped the papers into his jacket pocket, walked back to the lavatory and shredded them by hand into the toilet. Back in his seat, he watched the strange crab-shaped island approach, its pincers enclosing the azure waters of the Carribean. It wasn't until the plane was flying over the wretched shacks which surrounded the airport that he really began to take in the brilliantly colored landscape beyond. Then, stepping out of the plane, he felt as if he had walked into a steam bath. Under the malevolent scrutiny of several black giants in dark glasses with revolvers clearly visible under their thin shirts, he headed quickly for the air-conditioned terminal.

It was clear that the young president, "Bébé Doc" Duvalier, whose baby face was emblazoned on the façade of the terminal, had retained a private militia. Theoretically, his father's bloody-minded *Tontons Macoutes* had ceased to exist, but Bébé Doc had instituted his own battalion, curiously named *Les Léopards*. Jeff had to submit to a rigorous search and answer a mass of questions while a group of arrogant officials went through his baggage. When the ordeal was over, he sought out a taxi and told the driver, "L'Hôtel Villa Antillaise."

The road followed its picturesque and precipitous course to Pétionville. Jeff was so taken with the panoramic view over the bay and Port-au-Prince that he had the taxi stop on one of the hills while he got out to admire the landscape. It was there that the Haitian night made its sudden descent, projecting him into a primeval past — an African Middle Ages. A world of fear and mystery, of superstition and evil. The world of voodoo.

He got back into the car and asked the driver, "Can I hire you for a few days?"

"Yes, sir. Thirty dollars a day — the official rate. I will be at your service twenty-four hours a day."

Jeff made no attempt to bargain. He knew that with the reign of terror oppressing this strange country, the driver would not dare ask a penny more than the official price.

"Fine," he said. "But before we go to the hotel, I'd like to make a quick detour. Let's go by way of the Colline des Esprits."

The driver froze in his seat. His voice trembled. "No, sir. You can find another driver. I don't go to the Colline des Esprits. It's an evil place. A place of death."

"I'll give you an extra tip," Jeff said.

Beads of sweat covered the Haitian's forehead. "No," he said in a choked voice. "No, not that place."

Jeff gave up and fell back on the seat. "O.K. then, to the Villa Antillaise."

He was beginning to understand why they had killed Dennis Egleton on the Colline des Esprits.

"You see, Mr. Saunders, night rules us. Night is Haiti's real master. We are all its slaves."

Philippe Christophe, the proprietor, was a tall, well-built mulatto with graying hair. In his blue silk shirt and light-colored trousers and shoes, he looked younger than his sixty years. And his thick-lensed glasses and low cultivated voice made him seem more like an intellectual than a hotelkeeper. Following a tradition he had instituted more than twenty years before, he himself guided his guest to a table near the

lighted swimming pool and prepared his drink. Jeff told
him his first impressions of Haiti as he watched three grace-
ful young girls in white uniforms set the tables for dinner.

Christophe lit an American cigarette. "You are astonished
at the naïveté of all these people who believe in voodoo.
Look around you. By day, Haiti is gay, colorful, swarming
with life. But at night, it is voodoo. The country gives itself
up to phantoms and demons, good spirits, evil spirits. People are afraid to go near cemeteries for fear of encountering
zombies — the living dead. Ours is a country where the
gods fight against each other, where a person can disappear
mysteriously without anyone's being in the least surprised.
Here in Haiti, the casting of a spell can turn you into a goat,
a pig, a dog. You are nothing but a plaything in the hands
of the voodoo divinities and the sorcerers who know their
secrets. A pin stuck in a doll made to look like you can kill
you from a hundred miles away. They can put poison in
your food or scatter an aphrodisiac on your pillow. This is a
land of terror, Mr. Saunders."

Jeff protested: "Wait a minute, let's be sensible . . ."

Christophe smiled. "Sensible? Listen to the night sounds,
Mr. Saunders. Listen to the tom-toms, the songs, the
rhythms. These men's ancestors — they are also mine, remember — brought this cult from Africa. You say it's barbarous, absurd, that it's all superstition. Perhaps so. But
when five million men and women believe it with all their
souls, this superstition becomes reality. You can protest all
you like that a sorcerer cannot change a human being into a
black pig. But millions of people will swear they've seen it
with their own eyes. You don't believe it? That is your
right. But they believe it. Thousands of people hated our
dictator, 'Papa Doc' Duvalier. Thousands dreamed of assas-
sinating him. But a voodoo sorcerer claimed that only a

bullet made of gold could kill him. And since nobody owned a bullet made of gold, nobody ever tried to shoot him. Duvalier died in his bed. Have you heard about the rebellion that Duroc, our Minister of Defense, led against Duvalier? Duroc was forced to flee for his life. Somebody told the President that a voodoo sorcerer had changed Duroc into a dog to save his life. Do you know what happened? The next day, the Haitian Army received orders to shoot on sight any dog found in the streets."

"Mr. Christophe, do you believe in voodoo?" Jeff asked.

The proprietor's brief hesitation did not escape Saunders. "No, I don't believe in it," he said with an enigmatic smile. "But I have seen things that you Americans wouldn't believe. I have seen a small girl — the daughter of one of my staff — treated by the best doctors in Haiti. They gave up hope. Mambo Merimée came along and saved her life. I've seen a young woman who had just been told that a hougan — that is what we call our voodoo priests — had stuck pins in her photograph to make her die. She lost all desire to live. Two weeks later, she was dead."

Jeff started to speak but Christophe interrupted him. "Yes, I know, I know. You Americans always find psychological reasons for all these things. But here, we believe them. In the end, when everybody believes it, it doesn't much matter whether voodoo gods exist or not."

"That's an interesting philosophical observation," Jeff said, then shifted the subject. "Is it true that there are sometimes human sacrifices in voodoo ceremonies?"

"What did you say?" Christophe asked sharply. The three waitresses had stopped their work and were looking at him with their big black eyes.

"You understood me," Jeff said. "I said 'human sacrifices.'"

There was a tense silence. Finally Christophe put his glass down and said earnestly, "If you mean today, the answer is an absolute no." Then with sudden frankness, he added, "Look, I won't tell you obvious falsehoods. In the past, things did happen . . . horrible things. In the rebellion against the French . . . But that was a long time ago. Since the turn of the century, there has been nothing like that. The stories you hear were invented by writers trying to be sensational. Today, the most anyone sacrifices is a white rooster or a goat. There are no human sacrifices today."

"What exactly is a *cabri sans cornes?*" Jeff persisted.

Christophe looked straight at him. "It's the name given to the victim of a human sacrifice. It's an archaic term. I can assure you it isn't used anymore. But let's stop beating around the bush. I too heard about the body found on the Colline des Esprits. All of Haiti has been in a state of terror since that night. But I'm convinced that man wasn't killed during a voodoo ceremony."

Jeff tried to sound casual. "Have they identified him yet?"

"Not positively. Some people think it was an Australian named Roderick Brandon, an eccentric artist who's been lying in Port-au-Prince about a year. A few days ago, his servant told the police that his master hadn't been home for two weeks. The date of his disappearance corresponds very closely with that of the murder. But Brandon has been known to disappear for long periods. He sometimes visits the islands without telling anyone. In any event, it could be he. He was tall and thin, and Captain Cadet of the Port-au-Prince police told me the body was the same size as his. Actually, we first thought the victim was one of our guests, an English anthropologist named David Jennings. He also disappeared two weeks ago."

Jeff said evenly, "Yes, I read something of the sort, but I

didn't know he was staying here at your hotel. Later they said it wasn't him. Is he the one you mean?"

"Yes, that's right," Christophe said.

"Well, what happened? Has he come back?"

"No, he has vanished without a trace. The authorities have literally turned the island inside out in an attempt to find him. But nothing has turned up. I must admit the situation troubles me. He was an exceptional man."

Jeff kept prodding him. "Perhaps he went off to study some distant village?"

Christophe shook his head slowly. "No, they've gone through every village with a fine-tooth comb. He wasn't in any of the places he was accustomed to visit. But we're quite sure he hasn't left the island either. In any case, I haven't given up hope. I've kept all his things in his room on the second floor. I pray for his return, but . . ." He didn't finish the sentence.

"I suppose this is hard on the tourist trade?"

"To say the least." Christophe smiled sadly. "I'm sure your plane was more than half empty. My hotel is also almost empty. The tourists are leaving Haiti in droves. As a matter of fact, what brings you here, if I may be so bold? Are you on holiday?"

"No," Jeff said. "I'm here on business." He let it go at that, glanced at his watch and rose to his feet. "I'd like to have a look at some of the art galleries in Port-au-Prince. Is it too late?"

"No. On Saturdays, the galleries stay open late into the evening. They always hope they'll catch some tourist coming out of the voodoo show at the Habitation Leclerc."

"The murder took place on a Saturday night too, didn't it?" Jeff said casually.

Christophe eyed him quickly. "Yes, Saturday is consecrated to the most terrifying voodoo god, Baron Samedi."

Jeff couldn't be sure, but he thought he caught a note of distress — or was it perhaps a warning? — in the proprietor's voice.

It was twenty minutes past eight when Saunders entered the Tapis Rouge Gallery. He glanced indifferently at the naïve brightly colored paintings and the stylized mahogany sculptures. An aging Haitian lady with a broad smile approached him. "Can I do anything for you, sir?"

"I am Jeff Saunders." As he introduced himself, he showed her his card which she examined attentively. "From the Bates Stores. We have a large chain of discount stores along the east coast of the United States. We're thinking of launching a line of art objects on the theme 'Art everyone can afford.' We'd like to buy a sizable group of low-priced paintings for a special promotion in our stores; we thought Haitian art might be a good place to begin. Your naïve painters are very much in style at the moment. We were told that we might find a good selection here at reasonable prices."

She listened carefully. "Are you an art expert?"

"No," Jeff said quickly. "I am only a buyer, a plain businessman. That's exactly why they sent me. My boss was afraid that an expert might be overwhelmed by what he saw here and lose all commercial sense."

She smiled politely. "You keep mentioning inexpensive paintings. I'm not sure you will find many. The price of Haitian art has risen sharply in the last few years. Paintings by Préfet Duffaut, Casimir Laurent or Rigaud Benoit go for several thousand dollars now. On the other hand, if you wish to buy works by unknown artists, you can find some marvelous bargains. We are considered an artistic people.

Would you like to look at a few to get a general idea of their style and price?"

He tagged after her, examining the paintings as she pointed them out and expressing admiration at suitable intervals. He took careful notes of the artists' names and the prices. At last, having promised to return, he politely excused himself.

A half hour later, he went through the same act with the owners of the Centre d'Art, then at two of Georges Nader's four galleries. Everywhere, he was given earnest attention and indications of perfect trust. But the time had come to move on to more serious things.

It was almost ten o'clock when his chauffeur parked the car in front of 23 Rue Bonnefoix in the center of town. The street was dark. Here and there, a faint light shone from a shabby little bistro. Groups of blacks stood on corners, while others sat on the sidewalks. Jeff looked up at the lighted sign: GALLERY OF HAITIAN ART — BURT PARTRIDGE. He pushed open the glass door and walked in slowly.

"Good evening, I'm Burt Partridge." An American in his forties with a southern drawl and a wide smile walked up to him. "Welcome to my gallery."

Partridge was a large amiable-looking man, but despite his professional smile, his eyes remained cold and distant.

Jeff explained the reason for his visit, repeating his pitch about the "Bates chain of stores." Then he presented his card. Partridge examined it closely and scrutinized Saunders.

"May I see your passport?"

"I don't have it on me, but I would like to see yours. It's made out to Cassandra, I believe."

He hated the nonsense of code names, but it was an integral part of the profession.

Partridge nodded. "O.K. Let's go into my office where we can talk privately."

He locked the door of his small office, lowered the blinds and, without asking his guest, prepared two glasses of Scotch.

"We can talk freely here. The place is clean."

Jeff took a long look at the C.I.A.'s principal agent in Haiti. Partridge had served on the island for a dozen years. He spoke Creole perfectly and had a vast string of informers. His cover was foolproof: he was an authentic specialist in Haitian art, and no one suspected that his frequent trips around the island were anything more than a search for original works.

"You knew I was coming?" Jeff said.

"Yes, I was told this morning." He took a small notebook from his pocket and quickly leafed through it. "You've read my report on the murder?"

"Yes."

"Since then, there've been some new developments. The body has definitely been identified as that of the Australian, Roderick Brandon. He was supposed to be an amateur painter, though he never came to me. Have you any idea who he might be?"

"No," Jeff lied.

"It wouldn't surprise me if they found out his name wasn't Brandon at all and that he wasn't exactly an amateur painter either. My men and I have tried to get to the bottom of it, but so far we haven't found any indication that he was involved in clandestine activities or that he had suspicious contacts. Brandon had the reputation of being a loner. He had no close friends. I sent you his fingerprints even before the body was identified. Have you been able to attach a name to them?"

Jeff lied again. "No," he said without hesitation.

Partridge shrugged. "It's all pretty strange. As for the ritual murder business, I don't believe it. They don't make human sacrifices anymore."

Jeff glanced at a frightening funeral mask hanging on the wall. "I agree," he said slowly, without taking his eyes off the mahogany mask. "I'm sure you're right. Somebody killed Brandon and tried to pass it off as a voodoo sacrifice. They burned the body to confuse the investigators and cover their traces. The killer or killers knew how terrified the Haitians are of voodoo. They knew that the island would panic and that even the police would end up believing the man had been sacrificed to Baron Samedi. Before anyone dared go near the Colline des Esprits and start an investigation, the killers would have had plenty of time to leave the island."

"So you think the killers have left Haiti?" Partridge asked.

"Probably," Jeff said, rising to his feet. He appeared fascinated by the hollow eyes of the mask which seemed to watch his every movement.

"What could have been the motive for the crime?" Partridge continued.

Jeff didn't answer. He decided not to mention the Russians. But Partridge wasn't as obtuse as he pretended. "I'm convinced it was done by the Russians."

"Why the Russians?"

"That Englishman who disappeared from the Villa Antillaise. David Jennings." Partridge was now leaning against a small safe behind his desk. "I think he did it. And I think he did it for the Russians."

"How do you know?" Jeff asked, trying to control his excitement.

Partridge had anticipated his question. He handed him a telegram stamped in purple: HAITIAN POLICE — CRIMINAL

DIVISION — OCTOBER 26, "It's no longer a secret. One of my informants received the information from England. The news will undoubtedly be in the papers within the next day or two."

The telegram read:

PRELIMINARY INVESTIGATION OF DAVID JENNINGS BORN BIRMINGHAM JUNE 5 1915 VOLUNTEERED 11TH INTERNATIONAL BRIGADE IN SPAIN 1936–1938 STOP MEMBER OF COMMUNIST PARTY SYMPATHETIC TO USSR WAS IN MOSCOW LENINGRAD 1938–1940 STOP AFTER WORLD WAR STUDIED ANTHROPOLOGY CEASED ALL POLITICAL ACTIVITY STOP DETAILS TO FOLLOW STOP INVESTIGATION CONTINUES STOP CHIEF INSPECTOR SCRANTON SPECIAL BRANCH SCOTLAND YARD LONDON.

Jeff reread the telegram. "When did you receive this?"

"This morning. It all seems fairly clear. Our anthropologist was working for the Russians."

"Yes, your theory seems plausible enough," Jeff said. "But on the other hand, I don't think a man of his age, with his limited energy, could have done it alone."

"Of course he didn't do it alone," Partridge said with impatience. "Don't forget the Haitian who came to Father Finchley to announce the murder. He and others as well must have been in on it. Jennings, as an anthropologist, must have known all about voodoo and the evil reputation of the Colline des Esprits. It's my view that he used an operational team sent him by the Russians."

"But where are all those men now?" Jeff wasn't altogether convinced.

"They left the island under cover — as tourists, businessmen . . . As for the brains of the operation — Jennings — he must have left right after the assassination."

Jeff still looked skeptical. "I'm willing to accept the fact that Jennings was mixed up in the thing. I'm also willing to accept the fact that he did it for the Russians. But his disappearance seems to be too sudden, too strange. No one has been able to establish the slightest connection between him and the murder. Why should he run away? The Russians wouldn't get rid of a man like that so cheaply. The K.G.B. doesn't have men of his caliber to spare."

Jeff emptied his glass and stood up. "We can go on seeing each other without any trouble. Both our covers are solid. People will think we're doing business." He wrote out a few sentences on a piece of paper and handed it to Partridge. "I'd like you to get me the answers to these questions by to-morrow, if you can. Also, I think we should go together to the Colline des Esprits. We might turn up something."

Partridge started. "You think that's really necessary?"

Jeff looked at him with surprise and smiled. "Are you afraid of voodoo?"

"Of course not," Partridge said sharply. But the sudden nervousness had not gone unnoticed. Jeff turned solemn.

"In any case, we're in a nasty situation. Only one man — dead or alive — can provide us with the key to this mystery. And that is David Jennings."

The Villa Antillaise was completely dark when Jeff slipped between the heavy brocade draperies drawn across his door to the balcony outside. Climbing over the wooden railing, he dropped silently to the balcony below. He crept along a wide concrete ledge that skirted the second-floor rooms. When he arrived at the third room, he stopped and felt the door. He smiled; just as he had thought, it wasn't locked. He entered the room and carefully drew the curtains across the glass door. Only then did he turn on his flashlight. The bed was made. Two suitcases stood in a corner. The closet was full of clothes and the table was piled high with books.

He took a step forward and his foot hit something which fell with a dry thud onto the tile floor. He stood rigid for a moment, then leaned down to illumine the floor. What he saw astonished him. Leaning against the wall in a solid un-broken line were wooden statues, ritual masks, woodcuts in avocado wood and mahogany. All had one thing in com-mon: voodoo.

Moving on tiptoe, Jeff reached the desk and opened the top drawer. It was stuffed with papers — notes on Haitian customs and rites. The voodoo theme was everywhere. He rummaged through the other drawers with growing impa-tience. Notebooks, amateur drawings, quotations from legends and songs in what passed for Creole, all of it appear-ing to be authentic. They were the research materials of a practicing anthropologist.

In a bottom drawer, Jeff found several old letters from various English universities. He riffled through them. They all bore recent dates and dealt with Professor Jen-nings's research and the funds necessary for his "next trip" to Haiti.

Disappointed with his exploration of the desk, he started on the closet. With increasing urgency, Jeff felt the clothing that hung in the closet. He was leaning down to examine some lower shelves when the room was suddenly flooded with light. He leaped in fright.

"Don't move! Stay where you are!" He hadn't expected the voice — the musical voice of a woman trembling with fear.

He spun around.

Tall and slender, her arms held stiffly to her sides, the girl stood frozen before him. She had long black hair and large expressive eyes. She was wearing a white dressing gown and was obviously not armed.

Her shoulders started to shake as if she were about to cry,

and Jeff's fear quickly turned to compassion for this young woman who had dared the Haitian night to corner, un-armed, a burglar. "Don't be afraid," he said gently. "Don't be afraid. My name is Jeff Saunders. I won't hurt you."

"What are you doing here?" she said, still trembling.

"Don't be alarmed. I can explain everything."

"What are you looking for?"

"I am a friend of David Jennings's."

She drew back, her hand covering her mouth.

"You are not a friend of David Jennings's. I know his friends."

Saunders was afraid she might start to scream, which would put an end to the mission, to everything.

"Don't be afraid." He raised his arms. "Search me — I am not armed. I'll show you my papers. I work for the government, and I am here to help you. I want to find David Jennings."

She looked at him and a first sign of trust crossed her face.

"Who are you?" he asked.

She was silent for a long time. Finally she said, "I am Muriel Jennings. David Jennings's daughter."

7

Far away in the east, beyond the Cordillère de Saint-Domingue, the sky was tinged with pink.

Dawn was dissipating the pockets of mist in the narrow valleys, transforming the shadows of night into green hills, palm groves and plantations of bananas and avocados. It rekindled the vivid colors of the bougainvillaea, the blood-colored poincianas and the azure blue of the distant sea. Barking dogs, crowing roosters and children's laughter began to break the stillness. Soon, the Haitian women in gaily printed dresses would be walking with swinging hips along the road to Port-au-Prince, baskets of fruit and jars balanced on their heads.

"Now you know everything," Saunders said.

He was sitting next to Muriel Jennings by the side of the swimming pool under the spreading branches of a majestic poinciana. They had spent the remainder of the night there. She had told him about herself and her stay in Haiti. He had told her about his mission.

Of course he had lied. He had admitted to being an American agent investigating the death of the man whose

body had been found on the Colline des Esprits and who, he
believed, was connected with her father's disappearance.
But he hadn't mentioned the fact that the Australian Roderick Brandon was actually the spy Egleton. Nor had he
told her about his trip to England or the Crichton-Sloane affair. And he had carefully avoided any allusion to the fact
that he suspected her father of having organized the murder.

Did she believe him? He had the impression that he
hadn't completely convinced her, that some of the fear she
had felt at the beginning was still there. Even when she
began to talk about herself, there were hesitations, sudden
silences, a cautious framing of sentences lest something slip
out. They were like two poker players forced to show their
hands, laying their cards on the table one after the other
but still trying to hold something back and eyeing each other
with less than complete trust.

She spoke sparingly, avoiding his eyes in the semidarkness. Sitting slightly apart, she seemed lost in the contemplation of the swimming pool and the fireflies skimming
over the water. Only occasionally, when she threw her head
back, did he catch a flicker of light in her eyes. Elsewhere,
under other circumstances, he might have taken her hand in
his. Perhaps, in other circumstances, she would not have
resisted. But now she was confused and frightened. All he
could do was remain silent, listen and try to reassure her.

She described how her father had been the only son of a
middle-class English family, educated in the best schools.
An idealist and dreamer, he had been among the first to join
up with the International Brigades. He was ready to die for
the Republic in the Spanish Civil War. She spoke movingly
of his being wounded and his long convalescence in Europe,
and how his injuries had kept him out of the British Army in

World War II. He had become a professor of anthropology at the war's end and, accompanied by his wife, traveled to the four corners of the earth to pursue his research. Muriel had been born in Brazil, at Manaos on the Amazon River. She had gone on all their trips until they sent her back to school in England. "I lost my mother when I was seven," she said without looking up. "After that, I had only my father. The long separations were almost more than I could bear. To me, he is the most wonderful man in the world."

It had taken her a long time to choose a profession. She gave up her studies in English literature in the middle of her second year. For a while, she was the editor for art books in a large London publishing house. More recently, she had been given a part in a televised series on the B.B.C. She'd been so excited by this opportunity and the new horizons it opened up for her that she hadn't given her father a proper farewell before his departure for Haiti.

She had learned of his disappearance two weeks ago. In her despair. she had gone knocking on every door in London. "I didn't have enough money for the trip. I had to borrow on all sides. It wasn't until the day before yesterday that I had collected enough money. I arrived yesterday evening. They gave me a room next to Father's. I couldn't sleep. I heard a noise in his room and ran in. I thought that maybe . . . maybe he had returned. And I found you."

Jeff was silent for a moment.

"Did your father spend any time in Russia?"

"Yes, a few months. He spent his convalescence there after the Civil War. Why?"

He ducked the question.

"Your mother was Spanish, wasn't she?"

She looked at him with surprise. "Yes. But how did you guess?"

"From your looks. It's obvious that you aren't completely English. You say that your mother died when you were seven?"

"Yes," she said after a second's pause. Then she looked away.

The afternoon heat was oppressive. He knocked lightly on her door. She was ready. Without a word, she followed him across the shaded patio to the parking area. The chauffeur was waiting for them in the car, tipping his colorful straw hat over one ear and then the other as he looked at himself approvingly in the rearview mirror.

They drove along the main road to Kenscoff, then turned off onto a dirt road that twisted through the hills until it reached an intersection in the middle of a forest. There they left the car. It was ten minutes to four.

Jeff turned to the driver. "Go back to the hotel and wait for us there. We may have a ride back. But if we haven't returned by five-thirty sharp, come back and pick us up. Be sure you're on time."

"Yes, sir," the driver said solemnly. He examined his hat in the rearview mirror once more and set off in a cloud of dust.

At four o'clock precisely, a large metallic-blue Oldsmobile drew up in front of them. "Burt Partridge, Muriel Jennings." The two nodded without speaking.

"Do you have the answers to my questions?" Jeff asked pointblank.

Partridge nodded again.

The car started up the dusty slope. The last straw huts were left behind and they entered the jungle, bouncing along on the bumpy road. The forest formed a roof over their heads, and as they penetrated deeper, the sun's rays made their way only occasionally through the dense foliage.

Abruptly the tunnel came to an end. At first it had looked as if they were faced with an impenetrable wall. But a sharp turn led them between two hills. They were once again in the blinding light, winding between the steep barren slopes. Then they were surrounded by mountains and high peaks which cut off the sun's rays even in full daylight. The whole valley lay in oppressive shadow. Ahead loomed a large rock formation. It was bare, without a scrap of earth or so much as a plant clinging to its flanks. Partridge got out of the car and, without looking back, started to climb the path chiseled out of the stone. Muriel followed, with Jeff right behind her. From time to time, she turned around and looked at him anxiously. The climb took several minutes. Only once, Partridge stopped to point to the low lead-colored clouds that were spreading across the sky. "It's going to come down in buckets. It happens every day at this time of year."

They reached the summit. Unlike the arid, naked sides of the hill, the top was covered with hard-packed earth. The path led up to a small mound dotted with red candle stubs. Around them, the ground was covered with fragments of designs drawn in white chalk. In the middle of the mound stood a large cross of rough wood. Its horizontal board was thrust into the sleeves of a black frock coat and a bowler hat crowned the top of the cross. A death's head in white chalk was drawn at the foot. This was the altar of Baron Samedi, the god of the dead. A few steps to the right, someone had dug a shallow trench the length of a man's body.

"The Colline des Esprits," Partridge said.

"So this is where they found him?" Jeff crouched at the foot of the mound. Partridge knelt beside him and the two men carefully examined the ground. Muriel stood to one side nervously twisting a silk scarf.

Jeff asked again, "You have the answers to my questions?"

Partridge took a piece of paper from his pocket. He lowered his voice so that Muriel could not hear. "Brandon disappeared on October 14th, the day of the murder. The same day, Jennings vanished from his hotel."

"O.K. What else?"

"As for the local investigation . . . Well, when the police got here, there wasn't the slightest odor of a burned corpse. On the other hand, they did find the remains of a fire. Here, by the side of the trench, the earth had been burned. You can see for yourself, even though it has rained many times since. But they didn't find a trace of the goat the members of the voodoo sect claimed they sacrificed that night."

"No sign of a knife?"

"No."

"Have they fixed on the time of the murder?"

"The condition of the corpse made it difficult to establish with any precision. But apparently the members of the sect left around three o'clock in the morning — two hours or so before dawn. So the assassins had plenty of time to kill Brandon and bury him here."

Jeff leaned down to study the childish drawing of a snake at the foot of the mound.

"I just wanted to get a feel of the place," he said. "I don't think that Brandon was killed here. The murder was committed elsewhere. They brought the body and hid it in the forest or at the foot of the hill until the Haitians left. Then they climbed up, burned the corpse and buried it. They chose a good spot. Even in full daylight, it makes your flesh crawl. At night, they could be quite certain they wouldn't be disturbed. Their leader must have had a pretty macabre imagination to have picked out this place. I never thought the Russians went in for such flights of fancy."

"Why the Russians?" Partridge asked in a low voice. "In this whole thing, there's only one man who knew the secrets of voodoo . . ." He cast a significant look toward Muriel.

Jeff stood up and looked around him. The first drops of rain were beginning to fall. Partridge continued: "Tell me, do you think it was Jennings?"

Without replying, Jeff started to crouch again to examine the burned ground. Just at that moment, he heard a sound like the popping of a cork, followed by a rasping moan from Partridge.

He turned quickly, but only in time to see his companion buckle slowly at the knees and, his hand clutching at his chest, collapse at the foot of the mound.

Jeff threw himself at Muriel who was standing in a state of shock as she watched Partridge writhing. He grabbed her by the thighs and pulled her to the ground. "Get down!" he yelled in a voice he barely recognized as his own. "Flatten out and don't move!"

Muriel was on the verge of hysterics, her face contorted, her fists clenched to her forehead. Her screams split his eardrums as he crawled toward Partridge. The man's large body was twitching feebly, his arms and legs clawing at the air. It couldn't last much longer. By the time Jeff reached him, he had stopped moving.

Jeff felt his pulse. Muriel was still screaming, her face buried in the dirt. He quickly grabbed the crumpled paper in Partridge's hand, emptied his pockets and took the few pieces of paper and his small notebook. Then he got up and ran back to Muriel. He took her by the shoulders and shook her. She was still clutching the earth, her body

racked with sobs. He lifted her head and slapped her hard
once. Her crying stopped.

"Let's get out of here!" he said, his voice shaking with
anger. "The man is dead."

He dragged Muriel down the path carved out of the rock.
The rain had made it dangerously slippery, but Jeff didn't
slow down. Clutching his hand, Muriel slid after him, the
rain running down her face and mingling with her tears.
When they finally reached the car, she sank against the hood
and reached out to open the door.

"Don't touch it!" Jeff shouted. "Don't go near that car!"

Without another word, they continued on their frantic
course. Soon they were in the narrow passage between the
hills, then in the forest. Taking to the shoulder of the road,
they staggered along, stumbling and picking themselves up
in the thick vegetation. From time to time, Jeff jumped into
the middle of the road to examine the tire tracks while
Muriel waited meekly. Then he clambered back, grabbed
her hand and started off again, never slackening his pace
as the rain came down harder and harder in the growing
dark.

Soaked to the skin and up to their ankles in mud, they finally reached the crossroads. Muriel was gasping for
breath, her face scarlet. Jeff looked at his watch. He
shoved Muriel under the large leaves of a banana tree. "Try
to neaten up a bit," he said, breathing hard. She took a
comb out of her bag and tried to force it through her dripping hair.

Jeff too tried to put his clothes to rights. As the rented
car drove up a few minutes later, he put his arm around
Muriel under the banana tree. Trying to sound nonchalant,
Jeff said to the driver, "This didn't turn out to be such a
good day for a stroll. We sure are glad to see you."

Jeff put his jacket around Muriel's shaking shoulders and they got into the car. He didn't let go of her hand until they reached the hotel. Once there, he led her up to his room, sat her down on the bed and, with a towel from the bathroom, dried her face and hair. She was as docile as a child.

"Feel better now?" he asked.

"Yes." She looked at him gratefully.

"Now listen to me, Muriel. The dead man, Partridge, worked with me. I don't know where he was hit; there wasn't any blood. He was shot with a revolver or a rifle equipped with a silencer. I have an idea they were aiming at me. Partridge was standing most of the time while I was crouching. It wasn't until I stood up that they took aim. Partridge had just moved over to me when I suddenly knelt down. That's when they fired. And about the car: There were two reasons why I didn't want you to go near it. One, the killers may have booby-trapped it to explode when we got in. The other, Partridge's body will soon be discovered and we must in no way be implicated in the murder. If that happened, we might be held for questioning and it could take days, even weeks. If anyone asks you what we were doing this afternoon, just say we went for a walk in the forest. Is that clear?"

"Yes, I understand."

"Now, you saw me examining the road in the forest. A car took that road after we did and left before us. We were followed from the moment we left the hotel."

"What are we going to do now?" Her spirits had returned and she was trying to sound composed.

"First of all, I have to make a report about what happened. Then we have to wind up the investigation of your father as fast as possible. I don't think we're going to find him here. If he's still alive, he isn't on this island."

"If he's still alive?" Her eyes opened wide and began to fill with tears.

He nodded. "Yes, if he's still alive. Somebody wants to keep me from learning the truth, and you've got to help me. First, go to your room and tidy up. Then try to question all the people working in the hotel. Ask them about David Jennings. Don't forget that you're a girl looking for her father — that should work on their sympathy. They'll talk to you more willingly than to the police. Ask them about his habits; ask them if he received any mail, any telephone calls or if he had any visitors. Is that clear?"

"Yes, it's quite clear," she said and got up.

He gently touched her shoulder. "You have nothing to fear. If they wanted to kill you, they could have done it while you were standing on the hill. They didn't, so don't be afraid."

"I'm not afraid," she said, shrugging him off, and left the room.

Jeff picked up the telephone. "I want to call the United States." Fifteen minutes later, he had his connection.

"Bates Stores," a woman's voice said at the other end.

"Give me the imports department. I'm calling from abroad."

"Right away."

A cautious laconic voice came on the phone.

"Yes?"

"I'm calling from Haiti. You know about my business here?"

"Yes."

"Listen carefully. I've had some unexpected problems. I was just about to clinch a deal. I told you about it in my telegram this morning. I was about to sign a contract with an excellent exporter."

"Yes."

"But the guy pulled out of it at the last minute. Definitively."

"What do you mean by definitively?" For the first time, the voice sounded interested.

"I mean definitively. He's out of the running. We can't make any deals with him anymore. Is that clear?"

There was a moment's silence, then, "Yes, it's clear. That's very serious."

Jeff continued: "I want to know if you think I should contact his colleague. Maybe he could finalize the deal with me. Or do you want me to give the whole thing up?"

"Have you had any contacts with his colleague before this?"

"No. I've been dealing only with the boss."

"O.K. We'll call you back."

He heard the click of the receiver at the other end.

Jeff took a shower and changed his clothes. He was getting increasingly nervous. He poured himself a shot of whiskey and lit a panatela which he crushed out after a few puffs. He began to pace up and down the room. He couldn't rid himself of the picture of Burt Partridge sinking to the ground at his side. A man he had met only yesterday and who was dead today in his place.

He didn't have long to wait. He checked his watch as the phone rang. Just twenty minutes since his call to Washington.

"Mr. Saunders."

"Yes, speaking."

"One moment, please. Mr. Herter, from the American Embassy in Haiti."

A pleasant voice with a New England accent came on.

"Mr. Saunders? This is Jonathan Herter, the commercial

attaché at the embassy. We've just learned that you are here
to see about importing Haitian art into the United States."

"That's right."

"Could you come over and have a drink with me at the
embassy? We'd very much like to discuss this with you. We
might be able to help you."

"Thank you very much," Jeff said, and rushed out of the
hotel to his waiting car.

"The United States Embassy, please," he told the driver.

He was back at the hotel an hour and a half later. The
Haitian night had once again engulfed the island. Muriel
was waiting for him in his room. Her eyes were red, but
she showed no emotion.

"I did what I could," Jeff said to her. "Somebody has already set out for the Colline des Esprits. Partridge's body
will be found as if by chance. I've been given a new contact
but I doubt he'll be very useful. We've got to finish this investigation as quickly as possible. If nothing turns up here
in Haiti, we have to go look elsewhere."

"Go? Does that include me?"

"It includes you. If I go, leaving you here, then you become the prime target. Everything depends on what we
find out about your father. Did you learn anything from
the staff?"

She shrugged. "Nothing. Absolutely nothing. Father received no mail and no callers. He practically never used the
phone. He went on several trips to isolated villages around
the island, but he never once set foot in Port-au-Prince."

Jeff looked disappointed. "We're just treading water. We
haven't even the ghost of a clue. Did you talk to everyone?"

"Everyone except the concierge. He was out when I tried
to see him."

"I saw him on my way in. Come with me."

An old black man was sitting majestically behind the main desk. He was wearing a navy blue uniform with crossed keys in gilt embroidered on his lapels.

"Have you met Miss Jennings?" Jeff said in a respectful one. "She is the daughter of the Professor Jennings who disappeared."

The Haitian nodded sadly. "I am so deeply sorry, Miss Jennings. Your father was such a nice man . . . I do hope they find him soon. You know, he used to go off for several days at a time and always came back loaded with little statuettes and masks. He talked to me often, asking me about Haitian customs when I was a child."

"Do you remember the day he disappeared?"

The concierge shrugged. "More or less. He left early in the morning, in a small rented car he was driving himself. He always kept a bag with a change of clothes and a few toilet articles in the trunk, in case he had to spend the night in one of the villages. So far as I know, the car hasn't been found. Perhaps he became ill while on the trip and had to stay over in a village . . ."

Then he turned to Muriel. "Did you come directly from Spain?"

The question made her start. She answered, "No, directly from England." She was about to go when Jeff grabbed her arm and held her back.

"From Spain? Why Spain?" he asked the concierge with what he hoped was an ingratiating smile.

"Well," the old man said almost apologetically, "the professor mailed a letter to Spain nearly every day. I thought they were addressed to the young lady here."

Jeff leaned across the counter and seized the old man's hands. "Nearly every day, you say? Where in Spain? What town? To what name?"

Embarrassed, the concierge grew hesitant.

"Nearly every day, that is, until the last day. I don't know who the letters were addressed to, sir. I don't read the addresses. And I don't remember the name of the town. know it was Spain only because he always had to ask me how much a stamp to Spain cost. He was absent-minded, you know . . ."

Jeff turned to Muriel. "Do you know who these letters were addressed to?"

"No," she said, looking at him coldly.

They were turning to leave when a bellboy called him from the other end of the lobby. "Mr. Saunders! Someone at the entrance is asking for you."

Jeff went out. Muriel could see a car parked at the front of the hotel. A young man got out of the car, went up to Jeff and spoke to him briefly. He seemed very agitated.

Jeff swung around and raced back up the steps. He grasped Muriel's hand and pulled her after him.

"Let go of me!" she said between clenched teeth. "You keep dragging me around like an old rag doll."

"Shut up and follow me," he said sharply. "I have something to tell you."

He led her to an isolated corner of the large garden. He looked around cautiously, then said in a low voice, "I've just been told that Burt Partridge's body has been discovered and examined. He wasn't killed by an ordinary bullet. It was a projectile poisoned with cyanide, shot from a very special kind of gun."

She looked bewildered.

"Do you know the last time anyone was killed with a cyanide bullet? It was in 1959, in Munich. The victim was a Ukrainian leader in exile named Stepan Bandera. And the assassins were Soviet K.G.B. men."

He let out a deep sigh and ran his fingers through his

hair. "I hope you realize that we now have the K.G.B. on our tails. Like it or not, we are being hunted by the most cruel and deadly organization in the world. They aren't about to let us off easily. They're going to follow us, you and me, to the very end. Unless we give up before they manage to corner us, or unless we find the solution to this mystery."

Muriel still said nothing.

"And the solution is in your hands." Jeff's anger exploded. "You know damn well who your father was writing to. You know the address in Spain. His letters are our last hope. But instead you're playing games with me. You seem to enjoy hiding the truth when every minute counts. All right, Muriel. What's the address? This is a matter of life and death — yours, and maybe your father's."

She bit her lip. Jeff could sense the struggle going on inside her. Finally, she looked down and said, "He was sending the letters to El Rancho Nuevo, Pueblo de la Soledad, Province of Seville. To Isabella Guerrero."

Then she added, "She used to be called Isabella Jennings. She is my mother."

8

As THE DC8 CLIMBED over the blue waters of the Gulf of
Gonaïves, Jeff felt his stomach tighten with tension. The
mission had become a race against time. From the moment
Muriel has revealed her mother's address, he knew that
every minute counted. So he had to work with the speed of
light before the K.G.B. caught up with him again, before
they had him in the sights of their telescopic lenses.

From here on, he would follow extreme emergency proce-
dures. These had already authorized him to call on the
large reservoir of C.I.A. operational agents at the embassy in
Haiti. The United States used the island as an advance post
for its Cuban operations. Normally, Jeff didn't have the
right to contact them or to reveal his identity. His only
contact was supposed to be the chief of the local base, in this
case, Partridge. But with Partridge dead, he had to do everything in his power to carry out his mission and, most important, to get out of Haiti alive.

He had acted accordingly. Forty-five minutes after learning of Isabella Guerrero's existence, he had jumped out of
his rented car at the entrance to Duvalier Airport, with poor

Muriel close behind him. Three brawny "attachés" had
been dispatched by the U.S. Embassy to serve as human
shields in case the anonymous marksman at the Colline des
Esprits had a few cyanide bullets left over. Jeff was well
aware that his race through the terminal with the terrified
girl and his team of bodyguards was bound to blow his
cover. But that didn't matter now. Moreover, their precipitous departure from the Villa Antillaise a few hours after
Partridge's murder was bound to make them look suspicious. But that no longer mattered either. The masks had
been thrown aside on the Colline des Esprits, and from now
on the struggle between him and the Russians would be
waged in the open.

No one tried to stop them in the airport and they took the
next Pan Am flight to Puerto Rico.

Muriel lit a cigarette with studied care. She had waited
impatiently until the "No Smoking" sign went off. A stew-
ardess asked them if they wanted anything to drink. She
refused and turned away to look out the window. Outside it
was dark.

Jeff asked for a Scotch and soda, let down his folding
table, took a notebook from one pocket, a pen from another
and started to write. From time to time, he gazed vacantly
around the plane. His drink stood untouched on a corner
of the table. Finally he finished, closed the notebook and
slipped it back inside his pocket. With a deep sigh, he took a
large sip of whiskey and turned to Muriel.

"You lied to me, Muriel."

She glanced at him without answering.

"You pretended your mother was dead right up until we
found out your father was writing to her."

She drew herself up, the very picture of Spanish pride,
and said:

"And what about you, Mr. Saunders? Didn't you lie to me too?"

Jeff was unprepared for this. His discomfiture was apparent.

"You say you are trying to find my father. That you wish to save his life. I've never heard a more despicable lie. You don't give a damn about his life. Oh, certainly you're trying to find him, but only to get him hanged. You're convinced he was the one who killed that man on the Colline des Esprits, aren't you?"

Jeff shifted uncomfortably in his seat. She continued: "Do you take me for deaf and blind? You told me that the ritual sacrifice on the hill was only a farce, a camouflage, and that the Australian was killed by a Russian agent. Before he died, your friend Partridge told you that the assassin was clearly an expert on voodoo."

Her voice was heavy with sarcasm. "And you asked me — oh so casually — if my father had ever been in Russia. You, Mister Secret Agent, knew it all already. Of course my father had been in Russia. My father was a well-known Communist. And my father knew all the voodoo secrets. Therefore, my father was the assassin. And so you drag me everywhere to prove, with my cooperation, that David Jennings is a hired assassin."

"Muriel, keep your voice down, for God's sake!" Jeff said in her ear. Tears began to fill her eyes and she turned away to the window.

He was furious. As if he hadn't enemies enough already, now he had to take on Muriel Jennings. But for all his irritation, he knew she was right. He touched her arm.

"It's true, Muriel. I do suspect your father. You're convinced that it's impossible. You have confidence in your father. Nevertheless, you've followed me. And I'll tell you why: you want to know the truth too. You want to be certain that your father is innocent. But the truth may be even worse, Muriel. He may already be dead. He may also have been the victim of Brandon's and Partridge's murderers."

He pressed her hand. "Please, I need you. If you don't help me, we may never know what happened to David Jennings." She looked down. After a long silence, she was about to speak when the loudspeaker announced their imminent landing at San Juan Airport.

A black limousine was waiting for them outside the terminal, its motor running. Jeff and Muriel plunged into the car. A few miles from the airport, the driver stopped on a deserted road and they changed to an ordinary gray truck which took them back to the airport through the side entrance. Two young men were waiting for them next to a gate marked "No Entry." The truck was allowed through, their passports were stamped and they were ushered into the first-class compartment of Iberian Airlines Flight 411, destination Madrid. Jeff handed the two men the report he had written on the plane and prayed to God that Jim Sullivan would receive it in time to cable instructions to Madrid.

The plane was no sooner airborne than Muriel turned to Jeff. Her eyes avoided his.

"I owe you an explanation."

"I know."

"You asked me about my mother. I said that I lost her when I was young. That was true. I don't know if you'll understand. Probably the name Isabella Guerrero doesn't mean anything to you. But you must have heard of Dolores Ibarruri."

"La Pasionaria!"

"La Pasionaria," Muriel repeated.

Of course Jeff knew about Dolores Ibarruri. She had become a legend in her own time. Prophet and symbol of the Revolution, she was the flag bearer of the Communist soldiers in the Spanish Civil War. Small, with an iron determination, she cast a spell on the masses with her fiery speeches. At meetings, at the front, on the eve of battles, she managed the impossible: her faith and passionate harangues stirred the Republican soldiers to superhuman acts of bravery. Tens of thousands went into battle, her face before them. Many fell, her name on their lips.

"So you know the woman I'm talking about," Muriel continued. "But what you don't know is that there are those who say Dolores Ibarruri wasn't the only Pasionaria. They say that Spain had an even more inspiring woman, one even more venerated by the masses — Isabella Guerrero. My mother. She followed the men of the International Brigades into all their battles. She was the one who gave them courage to hold on during the defense of Madrid, the battles of Brunete and Teruel, the crossing of the Ebro."

Muriel spoke in a monotone, as if she were reciting a litany. "It was on the banks of the Ebro that she came to know David Jennings. It was love at first sight. The English volunteer of unshakable faith and the Spanish woman who had become a symbol of that faith. From that moment on, they never separated. At the end of the war when my father was wounded, they went to Moscow and lived there for over a year. Then she went back to England with him. They were married there, and she went with him on all his trips. She was an ardent, uncompromising Communist, with an almost religious belief in her convictions. That's what brought about the break. After the war, with the Russian occupation of Eastern Europe, the trials, the tortures and executions, my father began to question Communism. When Stalin's atrocities were revealed, my father couldn't take it anymore. And when the Russians crushed the Budapest revolt in 1956, he protested publicly and signed a manifesto denouncing the action."

Muriel opened her bag and took out a cigarette. Hands trembling, she lit it and inhaled deeply.

"My mother left him the next day. She had never questioned her Communist ideals. Her faith was as firm and unshakable as on the very first day. To her, my father had become a traitor. She didn't try to change his mind, but from then on, living with him was impossible. We woke up one morning and she was no longer there.

"But her life was in pieces. She was tired of wandering all over the earth, and she didn't want to spend her days conjuring up memories of the Civil War with aging exiled revolutionaries. She was a Spaniard first and foremost. Spain was her universe. She made an appeal to the Spanish Government, promising to give up all political activity. In exchange for her promise, Franco authorized her return to her native village. I don't think he believed her for a moment. But my mother was a good friend of Pablo Picasso's and I think Franco hoped that he would follow her example and return to his native country. And you can imagine how the Fascist propaganda machine exploited her return to prove that Franco had been right all along. In any event, that's the way things went. Ever since, she has lived alone in Soledad on her father's farm."

Jeff interrupted. "Your father never tried to get her to go back to him?"

"Oh, he went to Soledad several times. But she always refused to see him. She accepts me with reserve, and she never mentions him. He writes her almost every day — wherever he is — but she never answers him."

Muriel turned and looked squarely at Jeff for the first time. "So, that's the whole story. I didn't lie to you. It is true that my mother is alive. But I lost her many years ago."

As their plane came to a stop on the dark runway, Saunders stretched in his seat and tried to straighten out his clothes. He felt sore all over, his mouth was dry and the bitter taste of tobacco clung to his palate. He passed his hand over his face. He needed a shave, a hot shower and a few hours' sleep. He hadn't been able to close an eye after Muriel's recital. She had dozed fitfully from time to time, but mostly she'd sat staring silently ahead.

It was just past midnight when they entered the deserted airport. As they passed through customs, a young woman in a yellow Hertz uniform came up to them.

"Mr. Saunders? We received a Telex saying that you wished to rent a car."

He nodded. Thank God Sullivan had received his request in time. He handed the girl his credit card.

"All your papers are in order," she said in English with an unmistakably Castilian accent. "Please sign here. We have reserved a Volkswagen 1500 for you. You will find it right by the entrance in the space reserved for taxis. It is against regulations, but at this time of night they are not strictly enforced."

He signed the form, took the papers and the car keys. Outside, a night wind was blowing from the distant Guadarrama Mountains, bringing with it the heady smell of pine trees.

"Muriel, you do the driving. I'll give you directions." Muriel took her place behind the wheel without a murmur. As she started up the motor and maneuvered out onto the main road, Jeff took a black plastic folder from the glove compartment and began a minute inspection of its contents. He unfolded a map of Madrid on his lap and, consulting a typewritten sheet he found among the papers, indicated turns and directions to take as his eyes darted from sheet to map to street signs.

Muriel was a good driver. She knew Madrid well and, since Spanish was her native language, signs and indicators gave her no trouble. Once they had reached the suburb of Morales, Jeff said,

"Turn right at the first traffic light. Then right again. Calle del Silencio. Drive slowly."

She obeyed. They found themselves in a narrow dark two-way street flanked by low houses. In the distance, they could see the whitish light of neon signs at an intersection. Jeff rolled down the window in order to make out the numbers on the houses. "That's it!" he said at last. "Park in front of Number 38 and turn off the lights."

They waited in the car for five minutes. Not a soul was in sight. Not a single car drove by.

"Leave the keys in the switch and follow me."

They crossed the street to where a blue Seat 2100 was parked facing the opposite direction. The door was unlocked. This time Jeff took the wheel and Muriel sat down beside him. He ran his hand under the seat and found the keys. He started up the motor, turned on the headlights and, with a last look in the rearview mirror, drove down the street.

The roads were dark and deserted. A cold autumn wind whined in their ears as they set off toward the mountains of Andalusia.

Proud and eternal, Soledad rose before them, shrouded in the early morning mist. It was exactly as Muriel remembered. Nothing had changed since the day, five years earlier, when she had come to plead with her mother to rejoin the family and was met with a categorical refusal. And it was the same Soledad where, fifty-nine years earlier, Isabella — his only daughter — was born to José Guerrero. "El Pueblo Blanco" — the white village — the town was called because of the glistening white of its low Moorish houses and the high walls that enclosed its narrow twisting streets. Clinging to the slopes of the Sierra Morena, Soledad dominated the plains of Andalusia with its orchards of silvery olive trees and meager pastures. The southern sun would soon be beating down on the barren hills. Even at this time of year, its hot breath smothered the white houses and sent sad-eyed old men shuffling to the village café. Women in black with bent backs hugged the walls, then disappeared under the low arches of shaded porches. Soon the parched soil of Spain would shimmer in the torrid air, causing hills and trees to quiver as if seized with strange tremors.

But the sun had not yet risen, and the fresh grayness of dawn still hung over Soledad and the surrounding mountains. A lone shepherd in a wide-brimmed hat was leading his flock of scrawny sheep to the spring below the village. Two civil guards in olive drab coats and matadorlike hats paced back and forth, their hobnailed boots clicking on the paving stones. They stopped and eyed the Seat suspiciously as it halted at the edge of the village.

Jeff turned off the motor. "We'll walk from here."

The pure morning air felt refreshingly cool on their tired faces. As they walked toward the village, an extraordinary calm emanated from the countryside, binding them in a tacit understanding.

They finally arrived at a high white wall that enclosed a farm set a little apart from the other houses in the village. They stopped in front of a heavy wooden door. Instead of a knob, an iron ring hung from a short chain. Muriel grasped it and was about to bang it against the rough surface when the door swung open.

A tall well-built woman stood before them. She was dressed in black from head to foot, and her white hair was carefully combed and pulled back in a bun. Two deep furrows framed her molded lips and her strong jaw was slightly protruding. But most startling were her eyes. Looking into those deep black eyes with their extraordinary power, Jeff could well understand what had made men march to their death like heroes.

The woman looked at them haughtily.

"*Madre*," Muriel murmured.

An hour had passed since he'd been shown into the rustic dining room, and he was still alone. Isabella Guerrero had not shaken his hand. With an impressive, almost arrogant air, she had gestured toward the room, and indicated a massive stiff-backed chair with a leather seat which stood by a long table made of rough-hewn logs. She brought him a mug of strong coffee, a thick slice of black bread and a pat of fresh butter on a wooden plate. Then she disappeared with Muriel into a room at the rear of the house. Jeff ate his frugal breakfast ravenously, his eyes examining every object in the room — the large hearth black with soot, the chests of carved wood, the collars of red peppers drying by the window, the walls covered with layers of whitewash and buttressed by heavy oak beams. He knew he was an unwelcome stranger in this house, an intruder in a closed world. An aged servant came in and looked at him balefully, muttering to herself as she took away his dishes. Even the mangy Andalusian dog lying in front of the fireplace looked at him with suspicion and let out occasional menacing growls. From time to time, the voices of Muriel and her mother reached him from the other end of the house. Although Jeff understood Spanish well enough — a vestige of his several missions in the Caribbean — he couldn't make out anything of the women's animated conversation. All he caught was the difference in timbre between the two distant voices: Muriel's young and supplicating, her mother's deep and imperious.

At long last the voices stopped. He heard rapid steps in the hall and Muriel appeared at the door. Her eyes were red but she attempted a smile as she came over and sat down next to him. Her mother then entered, a large brown leather box in her hands. She placed it on the table in front of Jeff and looked at him.

"Here are the letters!" she said in English, and turned on her heels as if to underscore her disapproval.

But Jeff paid no attention to her departure, nor did he ask Muriel how she had managed to win her over. His entire attention was fastened on the large square box containing, as he now saw, hundreds of letters, hundreds of thin sheets covered with very fine writing. They were arranged in chronological order, and it didn't take him long to find what he was looking for. The most recent letters, those from Haiti, were on top of the pile. There were about twenty, all in English, each one beginning "My love," and all of them ending with protestations more suitable to an infatuated schoolboy than a middle-aged professor. Jeff felt uncomfortable under Muriel's watchful eye.

"Can I help you?" she asked.

"No," he said apologetically. "I'm looking for something special, a hidden, innocent reference that might escape you."

But the allusion was neither hidden nor innocent. He came across it almost immediately in a letter dated October 7 — a week before Jennings's disappearance. It read:

My love,

You'll never guess who I ran into today, here in Haiti, at the far ends of the earth and after thirty-five years. "Lolik!" You remember him — our "Lolik." Unbelievable, isn't it? I had gone to watch a cockfight in Pétionville, not far from my hotel, and there he was right across from me, sitting with a group of Haitians, cool and reserved as always. I waved at him and made quite a commotion, but I got no reaction. He must not have recognized me, which isn't very surprising. My baldness and glasses have changed me a good deal. He was sitting on the other side of the arena and I couldn't get through the crowd to him. When the cockfight was over and I finally reached where he'd been, he was gone and I haven't been able to find him since.

It's true that several decades have passed since we last saw each other, but I know it was Lolik. He too has changed since those terrible days on the Ebro and the splendid nights in Moscow and Leningrad. But his eyes are the same. I would have known him anywhere. I'm so very disappointed I couldn't catch up with him and talk to him . . . It plunged me back to my youth and that lost and forgotten world of dreams and battles. Perhaps I'll find him still. There aren't too many whites here and he may come to next Saturday's cockfight. But isn't is amazing to find Lolik after all these years and in such a place!

Jeff was certain he had found the key to the mystery. Lolik. Who could he possibly be? His hands trembled as he spread David Jennings's last three letters before him — those written after October 7. First he read them through quickly, then he reread them with greater care, word for word. But in vain. Not another word, not the smallest allusion to the mysterious Lolik.

"You have found something." Muriel, who had been watching him closely, noticed a change.

"Will you call your mother, please. I must speak to her."

She got up with some hesitation. He placed his hand on hers and tried to smile. "Muriel, he was not the murderer. I know that much now."

Her face suddenly brightened and she rushed to the room at the rear of the house. He returned to the letters and reread the October 7 one several times, then forced himself to read those that preceded it even though he knew he would find nothing. He was convinced that the letter of October 7 and the name Lolik contained the solution.

"You wish to speak with me?" Isabella's resonant voice interrupted his reflections. She was standing in front of him, clearly on guard.

"Would you be good enough to sit with us for a few moments?" Jeff's tone was both deferential and firm. She sat down opposite him.

"Señora Guerrero, I will try to be brief. I assume that your daughter has already told you the essential points. We are trying to find your husband. You know that he has disappeared. I wanted to see the letters he wrote you because I hoped to find some clue to his disappearance. It was an outside chance, but the only one I had left. I now think I've succeeded." He handed her the letter. "I believe that somehow his disappearance is linked to an unexpected meeting he had with someone. He wrote you that he saw an old acquaintance in Haiti. Probably an old friend you shared, named Lolik." He paused for a moment. "A few days later, David Jennings disappeared. Can you tell me who Lolik is?"

She looked at him without expression, not even glancing at the letter. After a long silence, she answered in a weary tone, "I'm sorry, Señor, I don't remember him." Then she stood up and, with rapid steps, vanished down the hall.

Muriel jumped up and started to run after her. But Jeff was already on his feet. "One moment," he said sharply. "I want to talk to her alone." He strode after Isabella and caught up with her just as she had entered her modest bed-

room. He slipped in and closed the door behind him. She
looked at him angrily.

"What right have you — "

"Please, stop this nonsense. Your husband's life is in
danger and every minute counts. This is not the moment to
stand on ceremony."

"He is not my husband," Isabella said.

Jeff sighed. "Señora Guerrero, I assure you that I take no
pleasure in prying into other people's private lives. But you
force me to go through this. Muriel told me why you left
your husband. I know that twenty years have passed since
then. But here, in your house, I have found the proof that
you still love him, that you care for him as much as you ever
did. I'm aware that you didn't answer his letters. But you
could have returned them unopened, or destroyed them.
Instead, you held on to them as if they were your most
precious possession. You guard them lovingly. A different
kind of woman might have tied them up in pink ribbons, but
that's not your style. You do still love him, don't you,
Señora Guerrero?"

She stared at him without speaking. For the first time, he
caught sight of the woman inside the legend. He saw the
pain and confusion in her dark eyes. Jeff continued:

"Until this morning, I was convinced that your husband
was a murderer. I was convinced that he had prepared and
executed that sordid murder in Haiti on Soviet orders.
Muriel must have told you about the discovery of the body.
Your husband disappeared the day of the murder. I
thought he had fled after committing the crime.

"But I've read his letter now. I don't know if you give a
damn about what I'm saying, Señora Guerrero, but I can tell
you one thing: David Jennings is innocent. David Jennings
did not run away after committing a crime. Something

quite different happened to him. By the purest chance, he
saw the murderer!"

Isabella Guerrero had turned deathly pale. She was
breathing heavily, but she still said nothing.

"I want you to understand what I'm saying," Jeff went on.
"One fine day, David Jennings happens to go to a cockfight
and sees somebody he recognizes. He waves to him. He
tries to catch up with him. After that, everything turns up-
side down. Lolik also saw Jennings. And he realized that
someone had recognized him. This was very serious, for
Lolik was undoubtedly in Haiti on a secret mission. My
guess is he came to the island in order to kill the Australian
whose body was found soon after. I don't know much about
it, but he obviously wasn't supposed to be recognized. Nobody was supposed to know who he was or even that he was
in Haiti. And that's why David Jennings disappeared. He
wasn't an assassin; he was a victim. The victim of innocent
memories thirty-five years old, brought back by a purely co-
incidental meeting."

She still didn't speak.

"You must tell me who Lolik is. Lolik is a Russian name
but I don't think that Lolik is a Russian. Your husband put
his name in quotation marks. Perhaps it was an alias, a nickname — I have no idea. You knew him in Spain, you were
friends of his in Russia. Until we find him and find out who
he is, we won't be able to learn what happened to your husband."

At last she spoke. The firm authoritarian tone in her
voice was gone. She was now a vulnerable woman.

"Why are you trying to deceive me? Of course I'm ready
to believe he saw Lolik and that is why he disappeared. But
when you say 'disappeared,' you are lying. You know the
truth as well as I do. We both know he is dead. He was
killed because he saw Lolik at that cockfight."

Neither of them had noticed that Muriel had entered the room and they both jumped when they heard her muffled cry: "Dead! *Madre,* you say he is dead!"

Isabella Guerrero put her arms around her daughter. "I'm afraid you'll never see your father again, Muriel."

"Maybe . . ." Jeff began.

"There is no maybe," Isabella said flatly. She had sagged against the wall, suddenly a broken old woman. "You know it as well as I do."

"But what about Lolik? Who is Lolik?"

She shrugged. "What difference does it make now?" Then, as suddenly, her manner changed. She straightened up, tucked back a stray lock of hair and eyed Jeff imperiously. "Besides, I don't remember who Lolik is."

He glared at her. "Why don't you say that you don't want to remember."

He was boiling over with rage. He turned to Muriel. "Come. There's no point staying here. That woman isn't going to lift her little finger for David Jennings."

Isabella Guerrero did not accompany them into the dusty courtyard of the Rancho Nuevo. She kissed Muriel goodbye at the door and threw a hostile glance at Jeff. But on the other hand she had said nothing when he took her husband's letter, folded it and placed it in his pocket. She watched them cross the sunlit courtyard toward the door in the wall. Muriel turned. *"Adios, madre,"* she murmured as if to herself.

Jeff raised the iron latch, pushed the door open and stood back to let Muriel through. As she passed him, he caught a glimmer of warmth in her green eyes.

And it was then that it happened. In a fraction of a second.

It was in that fraction of a second, as he was squinting into

the blinding sun, that he saw the black car on the other side
of the road. He guessed at rather than actually saw the
blackened barrel of the gun sticking out the rear window.
Before he even heard the burst of gunfire, he knew it was
too late. With a brutal thrust, he knocked Muriel to the
pavement and tried to flatten himself next to her.

The burning bullets hit him in the shoulder and the chest,
tearing his flesh. He had no time to feel the pain. The vio-
lence of the shock spun him around backward into the
white wall. The force of the impact ran the entire length of
his body. His face struck the rough stone and he tried to
clutch it with his nails, his hands, his body, but a red veil covered his eyes and his fingers slithered, leaving red stains on
the whitewash. His knees buckled and he collapsed on the
old paving stones of Soledad — an obscure village in the
Sierra Morena.

Part Three

Lolik

9

"HE'S WAKING UP," Jim Sullivan said.

Jeff Saunders shifted in the bed. His breathing became quicker, more irregular. He moved his head from side to side on his pillow. A cry of pain escaped as he tried to raise his left arm. Even opening his eyes was difficult and the impact of the sun's rays flooding the room made him wince. Slowly he became aware of blurred multicolored shadows shifting around him. Gradually his eyes began to focus and the fantastic shapes became white walls, furniture, people. Muriel's face emerged out of the milky haze. He felt her squeeze his hand.

"You are alive," he murmured. He barely made out his voice.

"So are you, Jeff," Sullivan said.

Jeff tried to turn his head toward the voice but Jim stood in the blinding light of the window. "Please, the light . . ." Jeff mumbled. Sullivan quickly let down the shade. Now he could see. Only Sullivan and Muriel were in the room.

He tried to smile. "Well anyway, it wasn't a cyanide bullet." He had found his voice.

Jim let out a dry laugh. "No, just a nice burst of good old nine-millimeter. Three bullets. One in your left shoulder one in your chest, one in the arm."

"Serious?"

Jim shook his head tentatively. "Not the wounds. Your heart and lungs weren't hit. One rib was slightly fractured But you lost a lot of blood, and for several days we didn' hold out much hope for you."

"For several days? How long have I been here? Where am I? In Spain? I have very important things to do . . ."

"Don't get excited." Sullivan's voice was calm but firm "The most important thing is that you're still alive. You're in the military hospital at the U.S. Marine base in Malaga You've been here a week. You'll be here at least a few more days. The mission can wait. Unless you want us to pu somebody else on it."

"You know damn well it's my mission," Jeff said with un expected force.

Sullivan gave him an odd look but said nothing.

Muriel was looking at the two men with astonishment "For God's sake, this man barely makes it back from death' door and all you can say to him is that when he's well he's to go right back! And you know perfectly well he hasn't dog's chance of coming out of it alive. He's followed every where. What is he? Bait on the end of a hook? A robot?"

"I suggest that we continue our conversation alone, Jeff," Sullivan said tersely. "Or maybe some other time . . ." He interrupted himself and glanced at Muriel.

"No, I want to discuss it now," Jeff said. "Muriel, pleas excuse us, but would you mind . . ."

"I like that!" In a fury, she crossed the room and slammed the door behind her.

Jim Sullivan watched her go and shrugged. "She's grown quite attached to you."

"No, no, she just doesn't like to be left out of things," Jeff said quickly. "Now, about this business. You really want me off it, Jim?"

"I'm not sure this is the moment to discuss it," Sullivan said, stretching out in the chair next to the bed. "You're still very weak. But you may be surprised to learn that I have no intention of taking you off the job."

"I sure am surprised, chief," Jeff said with his old sarcasm.

"Don't get me wrong now. They've got a bead on you, and I'm not in the habit of uselessly endangering the lives of my men. For all my feelings of friendship for you, I wouldn't hesitate for a moment to take you off the job if I thought it was necessary. But this is different. I don't think the Russians have caught up with us yet. They don't know if you're alive or dead. All they know is that Jeff Saunders was last seen in a pool of blood on the pavement in Soledad. They're pretty damn sure you're either dead or seriously wounded, and they're undoubtedly thinking that even if you recover, we won't let you go on with this mission. No self-respecting service would. I happen to have first-hand information that hundreds of Soviet agents all over the world have been mobilized for the sole purpose of finding out which of our men is going to take over and continue the investigation. Great. Starting tomorrow, I'm going to throw in their eyes all the sand I can dig up. I've got teams going to London, Haiti and Soledad. If the K.G.B. want to have some fun, we'll be happy to provide them with suitable distractions. In the meantime, I'll have you whisked out the back door and you can pick up where you left off without their being any the wiser." Then he added quickly, "You know this case better than anybody. You've been living it from inside since the very beginning, and I want you to carry it through to the end. It's absolutely essential that we know who killed Egleton in Haiti."

Jeff looked at him with surprise. "And here I was expec
ing to get holy hell for investing so many people's time an
effort in an operation that, let's face it, primarily concern
the British."

"Well, not altogether, Jeff. True, the British involvemen
was diminished considerably when Egleton's killers informe
them of the pseudo-ritual murder — or, in other word
when the Russians let the British know they were quits. N
Jeff, something much more serious is going on her
There's somebody in Djerdjinski Square who is ready t
move heaven and earth to keep you from carrying out you
investigation. Why? What are they so damned afraid o
What is the big secret they're scared you'll uncover?" Sull
van leaned toward Saunders. "Jeff, I've spent most of m
life fighting the Russians. It's been a good fifteen year
since they resorted to tactics like these. Every K.G.B. post
on the alert. Why? You'd think once their 'Mokroye Delo'
killers had picked off Egleton in Haiti, they'd consider th
matter finished. They'd go home and close the dossie
The man is dead, the traitor punished and the English in
formed. The End. But no! You arrive on the scene tw
weeks later and within twenty-four hours they try to shoo
you full of cyanide. Why? Then you arrive in Spain an
ten hours later, they blast you with a submachine gun
Why? What's behind Egleton's death? All I know is tha
they're busier than a pack of hound dogs. Our agents ar
drowning us in information on the subject. It's as if for th
past few weeks the only thing the K.G.B. had on its min
was getting Saunders!"

"About Lolik," Jeff interrupted weakly. "I haven't tol
you yet about . . ."

* Mokroye Delo: the department in charge of the K.G.B.'s violent oper
tions

"I know all about it," Sullivan said. "We've interrogated Muriel, and we found the Jennings letter in your pocket. That's exactly it, Jeff. Lolik. Who the hell is Lolik? The killer in Haiti was a Soviet agent. That's obvious. But why is it so important that nobody discover his identity? In all my experience, I've never seen the K.G.B. send a whole team of assassins across half the world just to protect an agent's cover. I wouldn't do it for any of my men, I can tell you. So who is this Lolik? We've got to find that out, Jeff. I think it's a lot more important than the Egleton business. This is really something big . . ."

Jeff was silent. His brain was numb from the heavy doses of medication and pain relievers he'd been given. But he had little difficulty following his chief's analysis and the new light he was shedding on the affair.

"Maybe Jennings . . ." he began.

"Jennings is dead, Jeff." Sullivan looked solemn. He pulled a cable from his pocket. "This arrived this morning. It's now official. His body was found in Haiti."

"Where?" Even though he'd known it deep inside him from the start, the news was a body blow.

"He was found quite by accident. Some fishermen looking for crabs found his body wedged under a coral reef near Kyona Beach — about fifty miles from Port-au-Prince. To make sure the body didn't surface, they'd attached chains and weights to it. There were two bullet holes in his neck. No sign of torture. He probably didn't suffer."

"Does Muriel know?"

Sullivan nodded.

"There is a traitor among us," Jeff said suddenly. Groaning, he pulled himself into a sitting position. Sullivan walked to the window and glanced through the lace curtains.

Then he returned to Jeff's bedside, took a large white hand-kerchief from his pocket and mopped his forehead.

"What makes you say that? That's a very serious accusation, you know."

Jeff had a gleam in his eyes as he addressed his chief. "How else could the Russians catch up with me so quickly each time? I arrived in England with a Canadian identity. When I met the chiefs of Security Services, I scrupulously observed all the regulations for secrecy. Even if they'd spotted me there, they couldn't have followed me to Haiti. I went through New York, I changed identities and took several other precautions. My cover in Haiti was solid. Nobody was shadowing me. And in spite of it all, twenty-four hours after my arrival, they tried to shoot me on the Colline des Esprits. They knew exactly what I was doing, where, when and how."

"It's always possible that one of their men in Haiti found you out by accident — through Partridge, or Muriel, or somebody at the hotel," Sullivan said without much conviction.

Jeff looked skeptical. "All right, let's accept that for the sake of argument. But then how do you explain the ambush in Soledad? They couldn't have followed me there, God damn it. They didn't know Muriel and I were leaving for Spain. They would have lost track of us after Puerto Rico. But admitting even that they guessed I was going to Madrid . . . In line with your instructions, I left the Hertz car and took the one you'd had prepared for me. I drove all night. Nobody was following me. Nobody knew Muriel Jennings was leading me to Soledad that particular night. And yet an hour after I arrive in Soledad, the Russians produce a team of assassins." He gave Sullivan a questioning look. "It was the Russians, wasn't it, Jim?"

"Everything points to them," Sullivan agreed. "As far as we can make out, they waited outside the village until you were ready to leave Muriel's mother's house. They caught you coming out and left immediately after."

"I'm absolutely convinced they knew my plans," Jeff insisted. "They had exact information that could come only from the inside."

"Whom do you suspect?" Sullivan tried to sound casual. "Very few people know about your mission. There's me, the chief of operations, four or five employees in the departments involved. And that's all. Of course, I've kept your British friends informed, as you requested."

"I think the leak is coming from England. That's what Crichton-Sloane thought when I talked to him in London."

Sullivan remembered something and smiled. "By the way, I sent him a telegram of congratulations in your name yesterday."

Jeff looked confused, then he broke out in a wide grin. "Did he finally get the post?"

"As of yesterday, he is Foreign Secretary in Her Majesty's Government. Old Anthony Ashcroft finally retired and Crichton-Sloane succeeded him as agreed."

"That's good news," Jeff said. "He really impressed me."

"Me too. He's the right man for them." Sullivan looked at his watch. "O.K. now. What are your plans?"

"I'm going underground, Jim."

Sullivan seemed unsurprised.

"No more telegrams," Jeff continued, "no more reports, either to the C.I.A. or to our British friends. From here on, I work alone. You'll be my only contact. I want a new identity tailored to my next moves. You personally paste my photograph in my new passport and you stamp it. You and I work out a new system of liaison. If I need the agency for any side operation, I'll let the right department know anonymously, using a special code you and I devise. As soon as I'm well, you get me out of here in secret. Nobody's to know I've left. Put somebody else in my room, increase the surveillance and see that somebody in the service comes and visits here regularly."

Sullivan listened carefully. "Very good. It's just about what I was going to suggest myself. This afternoon, when you feel a little better, we'll work out the details . . . But what about Muriel? What do we do about her?"

Jeff thought for a moment. "I'll talk to her."

"O.K., Jeff." Sullivan started for the door. "I'm with you all the way on this. I don't need to tell you you're getting into the most dangerous mission of your career."

Jeff laughed weakly. "I'm already in it up to my neck . . ."

He was finishing his first breakfast since his recovery when Muriel entered the room, a huge bouquet of red roses in her arms. She walked up to his bed. "May I?" she said with a mixture of timidity and guile, and kissed him on the cheek. He gave her a quick hug. She sat down next to him and took his hand.

"You're a changed woman," he said, with a broad smile. "Have you buried the hatchet?"

She blushed. "If it's all right with you." She then became serious. "You know, Jeff, sometimes small things lead to big changes. I'm not a little girl anymore, and I'm not naïve. I know whom you've been looking for. It's not David Jennings but the killers on the Colline des Esprits. All the same, I'm very grateful for what you said to me in Soledad, after you read my father's letters. You told me, 'He was not the murderer, Muriel.' You were direct and I felt it came straight from the heart. I knew then you were an ally and not the enemy."

Jeff felt embarrassed, as he always did when faced with feminine sentimentality. With Muriel he had gotten used to their adversary roles and now his opponent had suddenly turned into a woman. And, on top of that, a woman capable of turning his head.

She sensed his discomfiture and came to the rescue. "Not to mention the fact that you saved my life in Soledad. If you hadn't thrown me to the ground, I'd be the one in this bed and not you, or perhaps even . . ."

She stopped and they were both silent. Muriel watched him out of the corner of her eye and shifted in her chair. Jeff guessed she wanted to say something and didn't know how. Finally she summoned up her courage. "I'm very sorry about what happened in Soledad, Jeff. I mean before the shooting . . . at my mother's. I know she let you down, saying that she didn't remember Lolik."

Jeff had no desire to reopen that wound. He tried to sound conciliatory. "I believe she remembered him very well, Muriel. She couldn't *not* remember him. He was a comrade-in-arms—to both your mother and father. They spent a year together in Moscow. She simply didn't want to tell us who he was because, even today, she's not about to betray her old comrades or deny her Communist convictions. To reveal Lolik's identity would be like handing him over to the enemy. Your mother is a strong woman. Once she decides not to say something, nothing on earth is going to change her mind."

"She also knew that even if we learned the truth about Lolik, it wouldn't bring my father back," Muriel added.

He touched her hand. "Jim told me. I'm very, very sorry."

A bitter look crossed her face. "I expected it. After reading that letter in Soledad, I knew there was no hope. But I'd like to know who did it, Jeff. I had a long talk with Jim Sullivan today. He tried to explain to me why you had to continue with this mission. I wasn't convinced. But I want to come with you anyway. I want to be there at the end."

"It's impossible, Muriel. This is as far as you can go."

Her dejection touched him. He spoke more gently. "You can't come with me. From now on I've got to act alone. I'm sorry but that's the way it is. You don't understand the K.G.B., Muriel. It's an enormous machine with thousands of eyes, ears, spies, listening posts, double agents . . ."

She started to speak but he stopped her.

"But you can do one thing for me. Stay with your mother. Jim will see that the house is guarded. You'll be safe in Soledad. Wait for me there. And I promise that the moment I know what's hidden behind these murders, the moment I've discovered Lolik's identity, I'll call you. You'll have your seat in the front row for the last act of this nightmare."

Muriel sat in stubborn silence.

"You go now," Jeff said, patting her knee. "Jim Sullivan will see that you're in Soledad by tonight."

She rose and bent over him. Hesitantly. She touched his face with the tips of her fingers.

"Be careful," she said. "Take care of yourself. I've lost a mother, and my father is dead. I don't know you well enough yet to lose you too."

Then she left almost at a run.

"Union des Anciens Combattants des Brigades Internationales" was written in French on the flaking surface of the door. The office consisted of one shabby room with yellowing wallpaper, cheap steel cabinets, two tables and a few broken-down chairs. Some posters dating back to the Spanish Civil War hung on one of the walls; on another, emblems of the various regiments of the International Brigades. Enlarged photographs of Dolores Ibarruri, Tom Wintringham and Ludwig Wren hung on another. Opposite the door, above a fading portrait of the Republican leader Celestino Alfonso, ran the inscription: "Were it to be done again, I'd still be the first to go" — the last words written by the Spanish hero before he was executed by Franco's men.

The small gray-haired man sitting behind the table examined his visitor. "So you are the son of Jonathan Keynes?" he said in French.

"The very same," the young man answered as he sat down on one of the rickety chairs and placed a thin attaché case on the table. "Jonathan Keynes, Junior."

"Ah, that 'junior' is very American, is it not?" the old man said. "We don't have the tradition of naming our sons after their fathers."

"My father was killed during the landing at Guadalcanal in the Pacific," Keynes explained. "It was a month before I was born. So my mother named me after him."

"And where did you learn to speak French so well?" The tone remained friendly but the eyes were searching.

"I was brought up in Switzerland. After the war, my mother got a job with the I.R.O., the organization in Geneva for aiding refugees. That is where I grew up. And you are Monsieur Marcellin?"

"Yes, Gaston Marcellin."

"I wrote to you from Los Angeles."

With studied care, Marcellin picked up a brown folder lying on the table and opened it. A lean man in his sixties, he held himself as taut as a spring. "Yes, we received your letter." He slowly read the sheet of paper he had taken from the folder. "You say here that you are a member of the party, as was your father."

"I am head of the Communist Party cell at the University of California at Los Angeles and assistant secretary of the San Diego section." He took several documents from his pocket, picked out a red card and held it out. Marcellin pushed it away, saying, "No, no, I believe you, comrade." But the young "comrade" had not missed the expert eye with which Marcellin scrutinized the card before protesting his confidence.

"You see," Marcellin said by way of excuse, "we do have to make sure about the identity of the people we help. Foreign espionage services, and all kinds of . . ." he cleared his throat, "imperialist elements try to infiltrate our ranks from time to time. Either to collect information about comrades scattered all over the world, or to use us for provocations. Franco is still after us; even today our organization remains one of the principal concerns of his secret services. To be sure, he is mainly interested in exiled Spaniards; the others don't frighten him anymore."

"I understand," Keynes said.

"Will you permit me one more question?" Marcellin looked at him with his piercing brown eyes. "Why did you join the party? It's not very large or very popular in the United States."

"At first, I think, it was out of loyalty to my father's memory. You know that he was party secretary in Los Angeles. But above all, it was Jefferson's influence."

"Henry Jefferson? The party's national secretary in the United States?"

Keynes nodded. "He was a close friend of my father's, from the time of the Spanish Civil War. In America, many

consider Jefferson a national hero. During the Second
World War, he fought in Europe and won the highest military honors. He came to visit us several times, after we returned to California from Switzerland. He told me about
my father, his life in Spain, the battles he took part in. My
father was a Marine in World War Two. He won the Medal
of Honor posthumously. Jefferson convinced me that my
duty was to carry on my father's struggle. He considered
him a symbol of heroism and faith in a better world. 'You
must be worthy of the name you bear,' he said. His advice
made a profound impression on me." Keynes smiled. "I
was only a child at the time. When I grew up, I came to it
by my own convictions. But that's another story."

"I understand . . ." Marcellin seemed satisfied with the
recital. He had no reason not to be. Jeff Saunders knew
that his story was sound. His papers, documents, membership card — all were perfectly authentic. Jonathan
Keynes, Jr. was indeed alive. Except that at this moment, he
was languishing in jail for "driving while intoxicated" on
Highway 101 outside San Francisco. His mother had died
recently. As for the secretary of the Communist Party in
Los Angeles who had signed the letter of introduction to the
"Union des Anciens Combattants des Brigades Internationales," he was none other than a C.I.A. agent who had
been planted in the party for the past ten years for exactly
such purposes — and others as well.

"Your membership in the Communist Party doesn't jeop-
ardize your work at the university?"

Jeff was not keen to see the conversation become mired in
a discussion of California party affairs.

"I make out all right," he said noncommittally.

Marcellin did not pursue the subject. "Good. Let's get on
with our business. You have come all the way to Paris and

your time is precious. You wrote me that you were writing a thesis on your father's life." He glanced at the letter again. "Yes, that would be in the history department at the university, where I believe you are a teacher as well?"

Saunders nodded.

"Before I can tell if I will be able to help you, I need a little information. Can you tell me briefly when your father arrived in Spain, where he was drafted, and where he fought?"

"He arrived in February 1937." Jeff took a sheaf of papers out of his attaché case. "He enlisted in the Fifteenth International Brigade. He was first posted to the British Battalion called 'Saklatvala' under the command of Tom Wintringham and Fred Copeman. Then he transferred to the American Abraham Lincoln Brigade commanded by Robert Merriman — the Tom Mooney Company. He arrived too late to take part in the battle of Jarama, but he fought in the Battle of Guadalajara in March. In August, he and a group of volunteers were transferred to André Marty's Twelfth Brigade. When Fred Copeman was wounded at Boadilla del Monte during the battle of Brunete and was replaced by Joe Hinks, my father was reassigned to the British Battalion with the rank of Assistant Chief of Staff. He then served for a while with the Canadian Mackenzie-Papineau Battalion. He returned to the Abraham Lincoln Brigade to take part in the great battle of Teruel in December. He was wounded there and couldn't make the Aragon campaign. Once he was well again, he was assigned to the new Canadian-American brigade called Lincoln-Washington and took part in the battle of the Ebro. He was one of the men who swam across the river. He was wounded again and spent two months in the hospital. In point of fact, that was the end of the war for him. He returned to America about a year after the evacuation of the International Brigades and married my mother. Less than two years later, he enlisted again, this time in the U.S. Marines. He was killed on the beach at Guadalcanal. And that's the whole story."

Marcellin had been taking notes on a scrap of paper. He now opened the steel cabinet and took out several thick folders. "Why don't you sit at the other table and look through these documents. They contain everything I have on the brigades you mentioned and some of the men who fought in them. I'm certain you'll find your father among them." Then he took a mimeographed sheet from one of the drawers. "Here is an almost complete list of the books written about the brigades. You'll find them at the Bibliothèque Nationale or at the Sorbonne."

"Good. I'll look through them." The efforts of Jeff's C.I.A. friends were paying off. From among the two thousand-odd American volunteers in the Spanish Civil War, they had managed to find the one man whose son not only provided Jeff with an excellent cover but, much more important, who had fought in the same brigades with David Jennings. If Lolik was a comrade-in-arms of the English anthropologist's, he also had to be one of Jonathan Keynes, Senior's.

"There's one other thing I'd like to ask you," Jeff ventured. "I'm looking for my father's friends as well — former members of the brigades. When I go home, I'll try to find all those who returned to the United States and are still living. But you have quite a few here in France too, don't you?"

"No, not all that many," Marcellin said in a tone of regret. "Several died during the war, others were liquidated by the Gestapo and the Vichy government. Still others have dis-

persed to the four corners. But I'll see that you get to meet
all those who are still here. Do you have any names?"

"A few. The ones who wrote to my father," Jeff answered
uneasily. "But it's not going to be easy. Very few used their
real names. They used what sound like nicknames. Spanish, Russian, you know . . ."

"Very true. It was the custom of the time. To use a *nom
de guerre*. For example, I was called Captain Fredo. I
suggest you first compare the names you have with the list of
volunteers who served with your father. Those you'll find
here," he said, tapping a folder. "Then, go to our cafés and
talk to the men. I'll alert them about you. They'll be glad to
talk to you."

He jotted down a list of cafés. "Start with the Catalan on
the rue Mouffetard. They go there often." And he added
with a disabused smile, "You'll see where all our faith and
heroism have led us."

Jeff made the rounds. At the Catalan, the Bistro des Anciens, at the Andalou, at the Colonel Roll and Chez l'Al-
sacien. There he found old Republicans in Basque berets,
eyes flashing with the ardor of the past, their proud faces
bristling with splendid mustaches. Gnarled hands that once
grasped the barrel of a submachine gun now leaned on in-
valids' canes, and mouths that had shouted *"No pasàran!"*
and hummed the "Quinto Regimento" and "Carmela" were
now reduced to quavering recollections of heroic times.
The old soldiers were gradually wasting away, forgotten and
unknown, clinging to life and to the dream that they might
one day "go back." Spaniards, Frenchmen, Poles, two or
three Englishmen, exiled Americans, an old Italian, even a
few white Russians. But they stood tall in spite of old age
and disillusionment, and their eyes still gleamed with hope.

He spent long hours in their company, telling them his story, reciting numbers, names, battles and campaigns lifted from the dossiers in Marcellin's office on the rue de la Huchette and from the books on library shelves. He threw out names, asked what had become of this one and that, making casual references to David Jennings and Tom Wintringham, dropping the name Lolik between references to Laszlo Rajk and Boris Pasternak — both heroes of the Spanish War. A few remembered Jennings. "A good soldier," they said, their eyes flitting back to the past. Many remembered Pasternak. Fewer had known Jonathan Keynes. Those who did invited him to drink an anisette to "your father's memory." Everybody remembered Wintringham, Rajk, Wren. But Lolik?

"Are you sure you have the name right? Lolik? Just Lolik and nothing else? From what country? What brigade? Which battalion?"

He would shrug his shoulders and go back over his story. And, one after the other, they'd shake their heads. "No, I never heard of him." "You know, people often used nicknames at the time . . ." "A Russian maybe? Or that Alsacian, yes, Wallerstein . . . No, no, he was killed at Teruel . . ." "Why don't you ask Rivière, the writer?"

Rivière. That name came up in every conversation. "Talk to Rivière. He'll know. He questioned all of us three years ago. He knows practically all the names in the old brigades."

"Who is Rivière?" he asked Marcellin in his dusty office. He'd been combing Paris for two weeks without results.

Marcellin wasn't enthusiastic. "He's clever enough," he said cautiously. "A professor of political science. He wrote what he called an 'objective' history of the brigades. His conclusions are totally false."

"What about his facts? His documentation?"

"His facts are generally correct," Marcellin admitted reluctantly. "His research was quite thorough. Perhaps he can help you — nobody knows as much about the brigades as he does. Go see him. He lives in a little house in Normandy, near Arromanches." He wrote down the address. "The Allies landed in France literally under his window, the day of his birth — June 6, 1944."

The sea was beating against the beach at Arromanches. Huge waves cresting with white foam rose menacingly out of the dark water, swept across the narrow ribbon of sand and crashed against the smooth rocks. A heavy December sky hung over the Normandy fields. The wind, damp, salty and biting, bent the tops of the trees and penetrated the heaviest winter clothing.

Hervé Rivière was leading the way along the goat path that followed the edge of the precipice to the summit of the cliff. He turned to say a few words to Jeff, but the roar of the wind carried his voice away toward the frozen fields. Rivière was so thin that his scraggly body looked as if it might snap in two. It has been his idea to take this walk, having talked and pored over documents for well over six hours. The day was fading and Jeff was impatient to return to Paris.

They came to a small inn, named not surprisingly Les Arromanches, which looked out over the raging sea. To Jeff's astonishment, the low-ceilinged room with its rough wooden tables and stools was full to bursting. The local peasants and workmen had finished their day's work and stopped off for a few glasses of Calvados. The two men found a table near the window.

"You are probably disappointed," Rivière said straight out.

His eyes avoided Jeff's as he played nervously with a box of matches. "But you mustn't lose hope. The fact that we didn't find any trace of your Lolik doesn't mean he doesn't exist. But I know I've never heard his name before. Neither as a real Christian name, nor as a *nom de guerre*. As you saw, we found David Jennings and all your father's other friends on my lists, but no Lolik. The only explanation I can think of is that Lolik must have been a nickname used by only a small group of his closest friends."

"But David Jennings also mentioned him in his letters to my father."

"Ah, wait a minute!" Rivière's eyes brightened. "David Jennings! Didn't he go to Russia after the war?"

"Yes, for about a year. Why?"

"You know that most of the seriously wounded in the International Brigades, as well as the more prominent Communist leaders, were transferred to Russia at the end of '38. Between '39 and '53, Stalin systematically liquidated dozens, even hundreds of Spanish War veterans. Their brand of communism was evidently not to his taste. But some of them survived. Especially the ones who went to the K.G.B. spy schools in Moscow and Leningrad — the K.G.B. was still called the G.P.U. then. Those men were sent back to the West just before the outbreak of World War Two to infiltrate the armies, political parties and ministries of their various countries. For quite a while, in some cases for as long as ten or fifteen years, the Soviets left them in peace. They gave them the time necessary to become settled in respectable jobs, so that their enlistment in the brigades would be forgiven as a youthful lark. The Russians had time to spare. Often enough, these hibernating agents even managed to erase all trace of their participation in the Spanish War or their stay in Moscow — until the day when, inevitably, a messenger from the K.G.B. knocked on their door and ordered them back into service."

"And you think Jennings was one of those? Are you sure?"

"Jennings was trained in an espionage school. There is no doubt about that. But I don't think they used him afterward because he turned against them. But since you mention his name, I'd like to ask you a question. You say that Lolik was a friend of both Jennings's and your father's. Did your father go to Moscow too?"

"From what you tell me, I can't be entirely sure," Saunders said carefully. "But I would think not . . ."

"Do you remember the dates of the letters Lolik wrote to your father? Were they before or after 1939?"

"After," Jeff said with assurance. "At the beginning of the forties."

Rivière looked at him for a long time and suddenly burst out laughing. "I don't want to scare you, Mr. Keynes, but it's very possible that your father was a Soviet agent. Let's go back: Jennings attended the espionage school in Moscow, Lolik was probably there too and that must be where he got his nickname. No doubt, Lolik was his code name for clandestine activities. Your father was tied to the two men. And when Lolik wrote to him, he signed with his code name." Rivière chuckled. "You are on the trail of a Communist spy!"

Jeff did not share his amusement. "All right. Let's admit that Lolik may have been trained as a spy in Moscow. How can I find him now?"

Rivière spread his hands in a gesture of impotence. "There, I can't help you. All I know is that in Spain — in addition to the really dedicated Soviet volunteers — there were several dozen Red Army officers serving as would-be dvisers to the Republicans. But their real function was to ecruit potential spies. Some of them accompanied the ucky recruits back to Moscow to supervise their training. One of them might know something, but naturally nobody will tell you anything. This Lolik may still be on the job."

"And yet . . ." Jeff persisted.

Rivière shrugged. "I can give you a list of most of the Russian officers who were involved in recruiting spies in Spain. Their names are no secret anyway. But I advise you not to write to them, or to go see them in Moscow. An excursion like that could easily cost you several years in Lubyanka Prison. And your party card will be as much use to you there as a handful of cow dung."

They paid their bill and went out into the stormy night.

Forty-eight hours later, Jeff was rereading the message from Jim Sullivan which he had received at his Paris mail drop. He deciphered it following the code they had worked out together.

We have examined your list. Of the twenty-one officers you cite, five are dead: Arkadieff, Serov, Beliaeff, Bakunin, Malinovski. Four are generals still serving in the Red Army: Julin, Arbatov, Blagonravov, Arikidze. Three have disappeared: Colonel Raskin, Major Golinki, Major Ismetkulov. No one knows whether they were executed, deported to concentration camps or went underground. Three are civilians, and militant members of the Communist Party: Susnov, Bender, Tchlenov. Six have retired: Generals Polianov, Anski, Major Taticheff and civilians Savunin, Kirov and Nekrassov. Very important: General Polianov probably belonged — I repeat — probably belonged to the G.P.U. from 1939 to 1946. He contacted us about two years ago to ask for asylum in the West. His request was turned down for two reasons: we are not interested — I repeat — not interested in information from that far back; secondly, he stipulated that we

get him out of Moscow with his aged wife. Very complicate
operation. But in line with your request, have given urgent i
structions that contact be re-established and that we try to g
him out at any price — I repeat — at any price.

10

THE MOSCOW SKY was exceptionally blue and the morning was bathed in a pale winter sun. And, as he had on every sunny winter morning for the last five years, General Lavrenti Vassilievitch Polianov, Retired, struggled into his fur coat, pulled on his black galoshes and set forth. His wife, Katya, was still asleep. He didn't want to wake her up. She would soon be going to the hospital for her daily dose of cobalt; just as well to let her have a few extra hours of sleep. At seventy-five, General Polianov no longer had a car. For five years he had been without his massive, shiny Tchaika, and, three years ago, they had deprived him of his modest Moskvitch. He knew he had lost his aura of sanctity. Perhaps it was because he had once been close to Nikita Khrushchev, or perhaps it was the scandal he had caused in the Party when he had asked that his wife be allowed to undergo treatments in the West. Whatever the reason, that's the way things were and, as a good Russian, he had learned to live with it.

He went on foot to Red Square. Moscow was covered with snow. Muffled in their heavy coats, women of the Municipal Street Brigade were sweeping the streets and shoveling the snow against the sidewalks. The snow glistened, pure and immaculate in the sun. The general loved these beautiful winter days. He loved to sit on one of the benches facing Lenin's tomb and watch the long line of citizens — sometimes there were foreigners among them — waiting patiently to pay their respects to the remains of Vladimir Ilyich Ulyanov. They came from the four corners of the vast country: pioneers from the farms and *Komsomols* from Moscow and Leningrad, Tatars from the Crimea, Ukrainians from the banks of the Dnieper, Cossacks from the Don, stunted Kirghiz, pot-bellied Georgians, Kazakhs with Asiatic features, their skin weather-beaten by the sun of the steppes. He watched them go in and come out and thought back to his youth and the long road he had traveled. He too had waited hours outside this tomb. And once — when was that? in 1955? 1956? — he had even had the honor and privilege of standing up there on the top, on the large terrace, behind the nation's leaders, to salute the giant May Day parade. But only once. And the years that had followed had seen many an illusion dashed, leaving painful scars on his soul.

He lit a cheap Tchernomorsk and carefully inhaled the smoke. Even though his health was good, he had been trying to smoke less. He had always been the healthiest and strongest member of his family. The many years of struggle, from the Revolution up to the end of the Second World War, had left his energies unimpaired. But now he was worried about Katya. She was gradually fading away, growing weaker every day. And he knew there was nothing he could do for her.

A group of visitors came out of the tomb and dispersed in all directions. Three slender schoolgirls, the red silk ker-

hief of the *Komsomols* around their necks, passed in front of
im. Their giggling and chattering was music to his ears
nd he watched them with a smile. At his age, he could per-
it himself to caress a pretty girl with his eyes without being
ccused of indecent intentions.

As he mused, he became aware that someone had sat
own on the bench to his right. He glanced at him casually.
he man looked like a provincial, probably from some little
wn or other. Thick-rimmed glasses rested on his wide
heeks. He was almost entirely bald. His oversized clothes
ung on him like a sack and his tie looked as if it had been
notted to last the entire length of his stay in Moscow. The
an nervously rummaged in his pockets for a cigarette,
und one, tried to light it, failed, then tried again. The
eneral thought he understood his agitation: he was un-
oubtedly some minor official in a distant region who had
een granted his first visit to Moscow and felt lost and alone
the vast capital. He felt sorry for the poor devil.

"So, you like our tomb?"

The man turned to him hesitantly and smiled. "The
mb? Ah, yes, it's handsome. Very handsome, comrade.
ll of Moscow . . . You know, it's my first visit here. Last
ight I went to the Bolshoi and saw Vlasova. A dream,
mrade, a real dream! We have good artists in our coun-
y." Then, with a rueful smile he added, "But who can af-
rd to visit all these great places?"

The man was off and there was no way of stopping him.
e moved closer to the general and the words poured forth.
ot a stone was left unturned: his life in Odessa, the lamin-
ting factory where he was head bookkeeper, his family, his
rothers, his wife and two children. "Now it's time for the
hotographs," the general said to himself. And so it was.
he man took a batch from his wallet and thrust them

under the general's nose. Polianov nodded politely and
made the proper admiring remarks.

"And what do you think of this one?" the stranger asked
suddenly. Something had changed in his tone of voice.
"That's my native village. Look at it!"

The general stiffened. His heart started beating
furiously. It was the torn half of a postcard, showing a few
houses by the edge of the sea. As if spellbound, the general
stared silently at the card. How long had it been? Two,
three years.

"It's your native village too, comrade," the stranger murmured. "Seredino, on the Black Sea."

Yes, that was the password. Seredino, on the Black Sea.

Without a word, the general took out his wallet and extracted the other half of the postcard now yellowed with age
and handed it to the stranger. The man put the two halves
together. They fit perfectly.

"I have a message for you," he said, gathering up his photographs. "You remember where you met them last time?"

"Yes."

"Today, at the same time."

He got up, bowed politely, and left.

At nine o'clock that same evening, General Polianov
leaned out over the parapet on Kalinin Bridge and studied
the frozen surface of the Moskva River. The weather had
changed; the snow was falling silently in large wet flakes
on the darkened city. Only an occasional homeward-
bound pedestrian passed him on the bridge. Offices and
stores had closed hours ago.

Someone stopped near him and leaned over the parapet
too. He took in the figure out of the corner of his eye. It
was an older woman muffled in a dark coat. A scarf was
tied around her head and she had on heavy galoshes.

"I have been sent by friends from Seredino," she said without looking at him. "I have no idea who you are. They've simply told me to ask you a few questions. Are you still interested in the arrangement?"

"Yes," he said, his heart beating uncontrollably.

"Now, there is one condition. We need a certain piece of information. If you can provide it, with all the details, the arrangement stands. If not, we are no longer interested."

"What information?"

"You'll be told at the next meeting." She paused, then went on. "We have another question. Does your wife have to be included in the arrangement? You know she makes it very difficult."

"She absolutely must be included," he said with emphasis. "I thought I explained all that before. The whole thing is for her, not for me. Without her, I bow out."

She took this calmly. "I just wanted to make everything perfectly clear. But you must know how hard it will be. Also it will take a little time. Be here in five days at nineteen o'clock. If nobody comes, return four days later at twenty o'clock, on Red Army Bridge under Budenny's statue. You know the precautions."

"Yes."

A feeling of terrible shame swept over him. That he, a soldier, a military leader, a Russian to his very marrow, who had helped build the most powerful Socialist state in the world, should now consider fleeing like an ordinary criminal! He felt a sudden need to tell this unknown woman that it was not disappointment, nor any bitterness he felt against the regime that made him want to desert to the West, that he had no wish to betray his country by giving away any secrets he was privy to. He wanted to tell her about Katya, his faithful companion and wife of fifty-five years, whose body was slowly being consumed by cancer. He wanted to tell her

that it was only in the desperate hope of saving Katya'
life — and after his country had refused to help her — tha
he had decided on flight. Only for Katya.

But the unfeeling stranger standing next to him rattle
off her questions with such dry precision that he resigne
himself to silence.

"We will contact you," she said at the end, and walke
away with measured steps.

General Polianov watched the river a few minutes longer
then slowly returned home. He had now passed the poin
of no return.

For two weeks, Rebecca and Leib Kaganovitch had bee
living in a state of euphoria. The long, humiliating an
painful struggle was about to end. They were on the thresh
old of a new life; the dream they had clung to for so man
decades was about to come true. They were going to Israel!

The six previous months had been a time of unbearabl
anxiety. Twice, Leib's brother had sent them the officia
form from Israel, stamped with all the proper seals, reques
ing that the government of the Union of Soviet Socialis
Republics allow Leib Kaganovitch and his wife "to join hin
and live with him in Israel." On the first occasion, th
Ovir * office in Kishinev had informed him that the reques
had been "misplaced." The second time, the official merel
said, "We will contact you." Six exasperating months ha
gone by.

Suddenly, two weeks ago, they received a telephone call
"Comrade Kaganovitch, will you please stop by the Ovir of
fices today." They had both gone, almost at a gallop. The
sat in the waiting room for two hours, and the official wh

---

* Ovir: The U.S.S.R.'s Department of Visas and Authorizations, run jointl
by the Ministry of the Interior and the K.G.B.

received them spent long minutes rummaging through a
stack of papers before finally blurting out, "Your request has
been granted."

They returned home in a trance, rushed to the nearest
bank and paid the price of freedom: 900 roubles a
head — 400 for the visa, and 500 for the right to waive their
Soviet citizenship. It was an enormous sum of money, but
they paid it out of their meager savings without a moment's
hesitation. They presented the properly stamped receipt at
Ovir and were handed their visas printed on a single pink
sheet. A clerk affixed their photographs, had them sign on
the dotted line and wrote out "Valid only for passage to
Israel." The next day, Leib Kaganovitch left for Moscow
and went to the Dutch Embassy, which had been represent-
ing Israel's interests ever since the Soviet Union had broken
off diplomatic relations with Jerusalem after the Six Day
War. His reception there was altogether different. A blond
and smiling secretary stamped an Israeli entry permit on the
pink sheet. That same evening, Kaganovitch returned to
Kishinev, weary to the bone but brimming with joy.

Then came the feverish preparations — feverish because
of their joy at finally leaving for Israel, but also out of fear
that any delay on their part might cost them their freedom.
Who knew what idea might pop into the head of a K.G.B.
official? And maybe somebody at the Kremlin might decide
to stop all emigration to Israel? They had given up their
apartment and sold their furniture at a quarter its worth to
pay for the trip. They went to the bank and bought the reg-
ulation amount of foreign currency — 100 dollars a person.
And lastly, they turned over to Ovir their *propiska*, or resi-
dence permit. As a result, they were now without home,
without identification card, without nationality. They had
paid a last visit to the old synagogue in Kishinev, and Leib

Kaganovitch had been unable to hold back his tears before
the Ark of the Covenant. Burdened with their old suitcases
and dozens of packages, they took the train for Moscow.

They couldn't know that their troubles were far from
over. They had not noticed the strange look on the Ovir
clerk's face when he stamped their papers. Nor had they
known that the moment they left his office, the clerk had
made straight for a phone and babbled a few words into the
receiver. Had they known, they would have thought nothing of it. Overcome with happiness, Rebecca and Leib
Kaganovitch arrived at the Moscow terminal.

Their only daughter Nathalie was waiting for them.
Together they went to her small studio apartment near
Kronstadt Square. Nathalie had prepared a feast and they
talked and talked. Nathalie and Rebecca cried and Leib
wasn't dry-eyed. That was indeed the Jews' bitter destiny:
tribulations, separations, suffering. A heavy load of suffering. But the next morning, they would be on the train to
Vienna. Then, Israel.

The hours ticked slowly by, sometimes gay, sometimes sad.
It was past eleven when they heard a knock at the door.
Nathalie went to open it. Her parents heard a muffled cry
and saw her back away in fear.

Four men stood in the doorway.

They shoved her aside and marched into the apartment.
One of the men held a revolver. Rebecca looked at him hor-
rified.

The man with the revolver searched through their effects
until he found the pouch in which they had carefully placed
their train tickets, money and the pink sheet. He gave it to
one of his assistants who left the apartment, gently closing
the door behind him.

"You can sit down now," said the man with the revolver.

"We'll be spending at least two days together. From now on, nobody enters or leaves this place."

Rebecca Kaganovitch dissolved in tears. She knew then that she would never set eyes on Israel.

The train to Vienna had stopped at Chop on the Russian-Hungarian border. The line of Jewish emigrants filed slowly by. There were about forty today, come from all parts of the U.S.S.R.: from Odessa, from Moscow, Tiflis, Kharkhov, Leningrad. Children, old people, young couples. Around them on the platform stood mountains of packages, cartons, suitcases held together with string The customs officials meticulously searched the smallest parcel. The line barely moved. Then came passport control.

"Kaganovitch," the young officer called out, looking up from the pink form. An aged couple stood before him: a gaunt, ashen-faced little woman and a tall heavy-set man whose eyes flitted nervously around him. On his head he wore the *yarmulke* of a practicing Jew. The officer looked again at the photographs on the pink sheet. No doubt about it: it was they all right. Unconcerned, he stamped the sheet with the exit seal and motioned the old couple toward the train to Vienna. The woman staggered as if she were drunk and put her hand to her heart. The officer glanced at her and shrugged. These kikes acted funny when you stamped their visas. What the hell was it about this Israel that made them get so worked up? He scratched his head and called out "Next!"

The train slowed down as it entered the Vienna station. The usual crowd of parents, friends and porters jostled each other on the platform. A group of officials from the Jewish agency stood to one side, waiting for the Soviet emigrants. Large baggage vans were lined up the length of the platform, ready for loading. In front of the station, two buses were parked, waiting to take the emigrants to their temporary shelter outside the city. After a day or two of rest and more formalities, they would take a night flight to Israel.

It would have taken a very sharp eye to spot the dozen men scattered in the crowd who were waiting neither for a cousin from the provinces nor a business associate. They hovered in pairs around each exit. One was reading a newspaper near a newsstand piled high with magazines and paperback books. Another was drinking a beer at a lunch counter. They paid no heed to the people who occasionally glanced in their direction. Had anyone tried to guess their real function, he would probably have taken them for Austrian plainclothes policemen. And, in fact, the authorities had greatly increased security measures in airports and railroad stations following the renewal of Arab terrorism in Europe.

Outside, three cars waited with motors running. Their drivers were at the wheel, ready to take off at an instant's notice.

Jeff Saunders was standing watch under one of the station's soot-covered arches. Nobody except the chief of the C.I.A. team on the platform knew he was there. The two men had met only a half hour before the train's arrival. Jeff had come straight from the airport. He had given the C.I.A. agent a handwritten note from Jim Sullivan and whispered the password.

"It worked," Jeff said to him. "They're on the train. You wait here and don't move. I'll get on the train and talk to them. Then they'll get off alone. As soon as you see them on the steps, they're all yours. You lead them out of the station and drive them to your base. I won't need them anymore. Even if something unexpected comes up, don't worry about me. I'll be all right. But I doubt anything will happen. According to my most recent information, the K.G.B. doesn't suspect anything yet. They have no idea about the substitution. O.K.?"

The C.I.A. agent repeated his instructions. Jeff gave a nod of assent.

So he waited, his hands clammy with excitement. He looked at the photograph once again. Was this really the man now in the train? Had the visas been faked convincingly? Or had the Russians screwed them up at the last moment? And would this man really bring him the key to the mystery and tell him Lolik's real name? Another thought obsessed him: as callous and cynical as his many years with the C.I.A. had made him, he knew he would find it hard to forgive himself for depriving an old Jewish couple of their liberty, of their right to die in the land of their ancestors. And he knew also that the substitution was going to cause very serious complications between his country and the Soviet Union, and even more with Israel for whom immigration was a source of life. Furthermore, this was a one-shot deal: neither he nor any other agent would ever again be able to use such a stratagem to get anyone out of Russia. Inevitably, the Israelis would scream to high heaven when they learned about this, and not without reason. General Polianov's defection ran the risk of compromising emigration from the Soviet Union and might become an instrument of propaganda for the Kremlin. And within the next few days, he would bet his bottom dollar that the chief of the C.I.A. would be receiving a stiff note from the President, giving him hell and forbidding him any such tricks in the future. Jeff could only hope that the final results would justify the questionable means he had had to resort to.

The train came to a stop. Jeff was sweating. "This is it,"
he said to himself. He ran onto the snow-covered platform
and leaped into the third car where the emigrants from the
Soviet Union were assembled. The corridor was crowded
with overexcited people gathering up their packages, clutching their children and propping up the old and infirm. The
more agile were already elbowing their way down the narrow corridor toward the exit, toward freedom.

Jeff labored against the current, excusing himself, smiling
broadly and maneuvering with his elbows. He peered into
the first compartment, then the second and the third. His
eyes darted from one face to the next, lingering over this
one, then that, comparing them, remembering the faces on
the photograph in his pocket. Another compartment, then
still another. Children in tears, old people, packages falling
apart.

Suddenly he saw them. They were standing at the far end
of the corridor. The tiny old woman looked frightened, and
the old man in the *yarmulke* was supporting her with great
tenderness. He reached them after a couple of skirmishes.
"Mr. Kaganovitch!"

The old man jumped. "Yes, yes, I am he."

"May I speak with you for a minute, please." Jeff knew
that Polianov understood English but nevertheless he enun-
ciated each word carefully. He showed them into a compartment and pulled the door closed. His throat was hoarse
with suppressed emotion.

"You have nothing to fear. I am a friend. You are General Lavrenti Polianov. And you are Madame Polianova.
We are expecting you. Everything is in order."

The couple relaxed. A hesitant smile spread over Katya
Polianova's face. "So can't we now get off?" the general
asked.

"One moment," Jeff said. "You remember the terms of the agreement?"

The general stiffened. "Yes."

"You were told what we wanted to know — the *quid pro quo* for letting you pass to the West."

"Yes," the general said. He was tense. His wife looked at him with consternation.

"She doesn't know about it," he said with some embarrassment.

"I want the information now, General Polianov. I came here especially to hear you give it. Who is Lolik? Who is the man you recruited in Spain and took back to Moscow in 1938? What is his real name? What's become of him?"

A look of suspicion passed over the general's face. "I will not say anything here. I will talk only in a safe place."

"It's now or never, General Polianov," Jeff said firmly. "We know you well. You've been our enemy for years. Once you're in a safe place, you may very well say nothing. Then we've lost our chance. So you've got to talk now. Here. I'm waiting."

"No," the old soldier said stubbornly. His wife gave him a look of panic.

"Look," Jeff said, pointing out the window to the men posted by the exits, and praying to God the general wouldn't see through the subterfuge. "You see those men? There — and over there? They are K.G.B. agents. We alerted them with an anonymous phone call. They have no idea what it's about. They are waiting. If you don't tell me what I came here to hear, I won't need you anymore, and I won't hesitate to turn you over to them. You know only too well what to expect once they get their hooks into you. I won't hesitate so much as a second, and you know it."

Something in Jeff's expression, in his tone of voice, got through to the old man.

"Yes, I believe you are quite capable of doing that," he said thoughtfully.

"So, General Polianov, who is Lolik?"

And the general told him.

11

THEY HAD TAKEN the ferry at Calais. Muriel was driving the rented Peugeot. "Passport control is less thorough at Dover," Jeff had explained. "They're very fussy at the airports." Muriel asked no questions. Jeff seemed very sure of himself. He had worked out his plan of action down to the last detail. The English customs officer glanced at the license plate on the car, asked to see the international insurance policy and stamped their two passports made out to Mr. and Mrs. Douglas Rogers from Worcester, Massachusetts. They abandoned the French car in the port parking lot and hired an unobtrusive dark blue Ford Cortina. A foreign car with a French license plate might attract attention and, with success so close at hand, Jeff was determined not to take any chances.

He dropped Muriel off at the Dover railway station. "You know what you're to do, right?" he asked for the third time. She smiled. "Trust me, Jeff." He started up the car and drove slowly off. There was no point in hurrying. He had the whole day before him.

A little before nine that night, Muriel entered the Three

Feathers at Chippenham in Gloucestershire. The pub was crowded. The sour smell of beer merged with the acrid smoke of cigarettes and pipe tobacco. Jeff was sitting in a corner before a plateful of untouched food. When he caught sight of her, he jumped up from his chair and hugged her. "At last! Did everything go all right?"

"Perfectly," she said with a wide smile. "Exactly as you requested." She glanced at his full plate. "You haven't touched your dinner."

He crushed his panatela in an ashtray already overflowing with cigar stubs. "Let's go," he said.

The night was cold and dry, with an icy wind blowing down from the hills. Jeff's car was parked behind the pub. They arrived at their destination in less than an hour.

A sentry box, apparently recently installed, stood just behind the heavy iron gate at the entrance to the driveway. The sentry appeared in the beam of their headlights. He walked up to the driver's side of the car and, turning on a powerful flashlight, trained it on the interior.

Jeff handed him his papers — real ones this time, not fakes. "This is Miss Muriel Jennings. I am Jeff Saunders."

"Are you expected?"

Jeff evaded the question. "Please announce us. I guarantee we will be received."

The sentry hesitated. "It is very late, sir. And if it isn't urgent . . ."

"Do as I say," Jeff interrupted with impatience. "Announce us, please."

The man went into the sentry box. A few moments later, he re-emerged and, without another word, opened the heavy gate.

The car drove up the steep driveway and came to a stop in front of the manor house's impressive entrance. From the top of the steps, a man watched them get out of the car. He waited, a rigid silhouette in the darkness, as they climbed the steps.

"Good evening, Mr. Crichton-Sloane," Jeff said. "May I present Miss Muriel Jennings. Forgive us for coming so late, but I did promise to report to you the moment my investigation was over."

"Good evening," Crichton-Sloane said quietly. "Do come in."

They followed him across the large cold hall with coats-of-arms and polished armor hanging on the walls. The paneled study was dark except for a lively fire in the stone fireplace which cast a reddish glow on the book shelves, the hunting prints and the dark velvet draperies.

Crichton-Sloane sat down behind his large oak desk and indicated two chairs opposite him. In his impeccably tailored velours smoking jacket and white silk shirt, he could easily have been one of the titled gentlemen staring down from their gilt frames.

"My wife has retired for the night," he said in his deep voice. "I hesitate to call her. Actually, I didn't expect visitors tonight."

"No, please don't disturb her," Jeff broke in quickly. "And, once again, please forgive us for this inopportune visit, but I had no choice. I have been forced to be very cautious of late. Had I let you know I was coming, someone might have found out and tried to prevent me from seeing you."

"It's been almost two months since I've had any news of you," Crichton-Sloane said almost reproachfully. "I had heard that you were seriously wounded in Spain, but since then, not a word. Even our service chiefs haven't known what became of you."

"You'll know the whole story tonight," Jeff said. "Tonight, I will make good two promises. I had promised you, sir, that I would solve the mystery of Dennis Egleton's murder. And," he said, turning to Muriel, "I promised you that you would be in on the last act, right up to the final curtain."

Crichton-Sloane smiled. "Like the end of a detective story," he said.

Jeff did not smile. "Quite true. It's now my turn to tell a story. But by way of prologue, may I say that the solution was right there for everyone to see from the very start. I myself knew most of the elements. But I was not able to draw the right conclusions. Nor were my superiors. We misinterpreted some of the deciding factors and so we constructed a false picture — exactly as our adversaries hoped we would. But yesterday morning, in a grubby train in the Vienna station, I met an old Russian general who was defecting to the West. And he gave me the answer to my question. He gave me a name. That's when I understood everything."

"And what did the general tell you?" Crichton-Sloane asked.

"He told me who Lolik was," Jeff replied.

"Lolik?" the Foreign Secretary frowned.

"You already know most of the story I'm going to tell you, but from a very different angle, I believe."

Crichton-Sloane gave him another puzzled look.

"My story is about a young English Communist named David Jennings. Muriel's father," and he nodded toward Muriel. "He landed in Spain toward the end of 1936, fought in the International Brigades in the Spanish Civil War and was seriously wounded during the Ebro crossing. At the end of 1938, he was sent to Russia to convalesce. His mistress, Isabella Guerrero, went with him. There they joined up with a group of fanatical young Communists — Spaniards, British, Americans, Germans and French.

They had been chosen for a very specific task: to become Soviet spies."

"My father was never a spy," Muriel broke in with vehemence.

"I know, Muriel," Jeff said in a conciliatory tone, "but let me get on with my story."

"I don't see how this . . ." Crichton-Sloane began.

Jeff ignored the interruption. "Once he was well again, David Jennings spent about a year in Moscow and Leningrad. He was initiated into the techniques of espionage and subversive activities at the K.G.B. training centers. For security reasons, the foreign students were organized in small closely knit cells. I have no idea how many there were in Jennings's and Isabella Guerrero's cell. In any event, they were not allowed to use their real names. Each one was given a *nom de guerre*. One of their group was given the name of Lolik. His real name won't mean much to you. It was Reginald Hawkes.

"When they left the Soviet Union, Jennings and Hawkes separated. They never saw each other again. I think it must have been at about this time that Jennings's Communist ardor began to cool. Or perhaps the Russians thought to use him later and decided to leave him to his own devices for a while. Whatever the reason, he was not put to work."

"He hated them . . ." Muriel blurted out.

"But there was Lolik," Jeff said patiently. "As a matter of fact, Lolik was singled out from the beginning by the Soviet intelligence services. He had distinguished himself during his training period, and his superiors thought he was destined for great things. First they devised a new identity for him, and erased all traces of his past in Spain and the U.S.S.R. World War Two had just broken out, and the heavy bombing of England made their task easy. Among the thousands killed during the German air raid on Coventry, the Soviet agents discovered a young man without family, without connections of any kind. Lolik and he were the same age. So Lolik had authentic papers made out in the name of the man killed during the air raid. Reginald Hawkes ceased to exist. Using his new name, he enlisted in the British Army and distinguished himself in combat. And you'd never guess Lolik's new name." He paused. "It was Dennis Harold Egleton."

"I don't believe it!" Crichton-Sloane stiffened with anger. "Your imagination is running away with you. What kind of rubbish is this, Saunders?"

Jeff was impassive. He lit a cigarillo and, leaning forward in his chair, spoke with cold precision: "Dennis Harold Egleton, born in Lewes, Sussex. Under that name, he carried out some of the most daring exploits in the history of the Royal Army's commando units. Under that name, he entered the British Secret Service in 1948. The Russians were right. His talents were soon recognized at M.I.6 — his instinct for clandestine activity and his knowledge of the enemy, meaning the Soviet Union." Jeff laughed unpleasantly. "And of course, he did know a thing or two about the Soviet Union . . ."

"You're mad!" Crichton-Sloane said, and half turned away.

Jeff shrugged and went on: "Now it was the turn of the British to train him for his future mission. It was obvious that a man of Egleton's stamp should be used as a double agent against the Soviets. His chiefs spared no effort. He was given a foolproof cover as a supplier of electronic equipment to the Royal Navy. In 1952, they sent him to Russia to establish contact with the Soviets, thus plunging headlong into the trap the Russians had set for them.

"So it wasn't exactly surprising that he was greeted with

open arms by Moscow and almost immediately entrusted with 'top-secret' intelligence. After all, wasn't he their man?" Jeff shook his head in disbelief. "I've kept asking myself how any of us — all you British and I, an American agent — could have believed for a moment that the Russians would furnish their agent in England with 'top-secret' intelligence. To what end?"

"As I was driving here, I went over these so-called secrets the Russians were supposed to have given Egleton — these great revelations that made your James Fleming and Brian Auchinleck so ecstatic. And I came to the realization that here were three kinds of information involved: what the West would sooner or later learn by itself — like, for example, the rupture between Peking and Moscow; what the U.S.S.R. wanted to have leak out — such as Khrushchev's speech on Stalin's crimes; and information that was nothing but pure fiction — like the strategic atomic weapons in the Soviet arsenal.

"The whole thing was a farce. The British thought they had an inspired super-agent through whom they could deluge the Russians with false information while they obtained priceless secrets in exchange. But the Soviets threw the false information in the wastebasket, obtained real information from the same agent and made the British swallow whatever they damn pleased."

Crichton-Sloane continued to sit in frozen silence, while Jeff, his voice growing hoarse, made no attempt to hide his contempt.

"Egleton, adviser on psychological warfare to the K.G.B.? Come on! The Russians aren't exactly amateurs where psychological warfare is concerned. They would never have entrusted him with such a role. Egleton was lying, of course. But the bosses at M.I.5 and M.I.6 had an almost mystical faith in him and swallowed all his guff without a murmur.

And why should they suspect him? Wasn't he their star double agent? Wasn't he the one who kept bringing them such valuable information while paying the Russians back with a lot of crap?

"I really do believe that Egleton deserves to be called the greatest postwar Soviet agent, and maybe even one of the greatest spies of our time. I wonder how long it will take England to recover from the damage he did over the past twenty years. I also wonder how much longer he could have gone on playing his double game. Many long years, perhaps, if something hadn't suddenly happened that brought his noteworthy career to an abrupt end."

He paused, waiting to see if Crichton-Sloane would react.

"And what did happen?" the Foreign Secretary asked with studied indifference.

"What happened is that you, sir, wrote that stupid letter."

One of the logs in the fire snapped in two, throwing sparks in all directions. Muriel jumped with fright, while Crichton-Sloane sprang from his chair.

"You're insane!" he shouted, his face contorted with rage. He leaped at Saunders, clutching his lapels and shaking him violently. "That's a damnable lie! I'll see that you pay for this!"

Jeff tried to free himself but his strength failed him. Panic-stricken, Muriel tried to separate the two men. "Let go of him, you bully!" she screamed, "you know he's been injured."

Crichton-Sloane shoved her aside. His face was covered with sweat.

"You'll pay for this!" His deep voice became menacing. "Malign me in my own house! You're playing their game! You're part of their filthy plot to destroy me!"

Jeff finally managed to push him off. "I had hoped for a more interesting response. I thought perhaps you'd show me the door, then head straight to the phone and get the U.S. ambassador out of bed."

Crichton-Sloane walked stiffly to the fireplace and turned toward Saunders. With a magisterial air, he said, "You are in the house of a member of Her Majesty's Government. Do not forget to whom you are speaking!"

Mimicking his tone, Jeff replied, "I am speaking to a Soviet agent who has succeeded in infiltrating Her Majesty's Government. And you, Mr. Secretary, are going to listen to my story to the very end. In fact you are extremely anxious to hear it, if only because you want to know exactly how much I know and what I've done about it."

He won his point. Crichton-Sloane silently returned to the chair behind his desk, sat down and folded his arms across his chest. Neither looked at Muriel who was sobbing quietly near the fireplace.

"Yes, you're the man who wrote that letter, all right," Saunders resumed. "Stanley Crichton-Sloane, Britain's great hope, tomorrow's leader. When did you become a Communist, Mr. Crichton-Sloane? In Newcastle, as a boy? As a frustrated miner in Wales? Or during your student days at Oxford? I don't know and I suppose it doesn't really matter. But I bet your name isn't on any list of Communist Party members. You are a lone wolf, a prudent lone wolf, Mr. Crichton-Sloane. Probably you've never even attended a single Communist meeting. And I also bet you can count on the fingers of one hand the number of K.G.B. members or Soviet officials who know that this ranking minister in Her Majesty's Government is a dedicated Communist, a man ready to betray his country for the sake of the Russians.

"You worked in the shadows, and that's where your Moscow friends wanted you. They didn't want to see you wasted on paltry assignments. They were very conscious of your enormous potential and wanted to push you to the summit of the hierarchy, to where you are now and maybe even higher. Prime Minister! It may seem fantastic — a Soviet agent as Prime Minister, but why not? What's an Egleton compared to you?"

Again Saunders paused, his eyes on Crichton-Sloane. But the Foreign Secretary continued to sit in stony silence. Jeff went on:

"When the Soviets spread their espionage network over England, it was you they picked to run it. No single agent of the K.G.B. in England knew of your existence. You received your instructions direct from Moscow. Only two people knew your identity: your liaison agents Manoli Theodoris and Sheila MacAlister. That is why when a hundred and five agents working for the K.G.B. were exposed and expelled from England, you had nothing to fear."

Crichton-Sloane rose from his chair and with a look of disdain walked over to the large French windows overlooking the park. He opened them wide and the cold wind blew into the room, making the curtains billow around the minister's motionless figure. From the distance came the sound of rustling leaves and the cry of night birds.

Jeff raised his voice to counter the intruding noise. "You felt quite secure, didn't you, until that morning when Sheila MacAlister came to you in a panic and announced she was in immediate danger of being arrested. This put you in a ticklish spot. She knew who you were. It was absolutely essential to get her out of England. You had to move with great speed and you held only one card in your hand. You knew that Theodoris was in Saint-Tropez. Your only recourse was to write him a letter in your own hand, on House of

Commons stationery, which you gave to Sheila MacAlister. Your handwriting and your name Stanley on the House of Commons letterhead were the only means you had to identify yourself to Theodoris. I suppose you made Sheila swear by Marx, Engels and Lenin that she wouldn't let herself be caught alive.

"What happened next was just plain bad coordination. The Russians didn't know Sheila was on her way to Saint-Tropez. All they knew was that their men in England were in desperate straits, that one of them might spill the beans and reveal Theodoris's role. So they decided to liquidate him. They dispatched one of their commando teams to France and shot him down on the deck of his yacht. When poor Sheila arrived on the scene, all she found was a corpse. And your letter fell into the hands of the police."

"Ridiculous," Crichton-Sloane spat over his shoulder.

Jeff continued unconcerned: "It was a harsh blow, but heaven came to your rescue. Sheila committed suicide. There was nobody left who could prove you had given her the letter. When the news made the front pages, you could deny it without a worry in the world. Which of course you did — and very skillfully too. Meanwhile, your Moscow friends concocted a last-ditch plot to save you. After all, weren't you their most precious possession in the West? They were ready to do anything to get you off the hook, even to sacrificing the best double agent they ever had — Egleton. The K.G.B. cleverly exploited the fact that Moscow had never missed an opportunity to throw mud at you, making you out to be a ferocious anti-Communist. So they have poor Egleton flying to England and turning up at James Fleming's in the middle of the night. He tells the head of M.I.6 that the letter was a vile plot engineered by the Russians to demolish you once and for all and bring

your political career to an end. He tells him that Theodoris's assassination was set up so that Sheila would be arrested with the letter in her hand. And that it was he, Egleton himself, who drafted the letter which was then
counterfeited by K.G.B. experts. He also says that the letter
was given to Sheila by a Soviet liaison agent named Kolodni."

Jeff let out an appreciative chuckle. "The British swallowed Egleton's story hook, line and sinker, even though
they never managed to find out where or how this Kolodni
made contact with Sheila. It's my own theory that Kolodni
wasn't even a secret agent. The K.G.B. simply decided to
use the name of any Soviet official who happened to arrive
in London on September 18th.

"The K.G.B. maneuver worked like a dream. You were
absolved. Better yet: all England was conscience-stricken and
asked your forgiveness for having suspected you. In their
gratitude, the British Secret Service worked out a plan for
Egleton: he was to be brought to justice, but he would suffer
a fake heart attack in the dock and they would secretly whisk
him out of England. Given a new identity, he would be sent
to Haiti to start a new life. And so the coffin buried at the
cemetery in Lewes was empty."

There was a sudden muffled cry behind them that made
all three jump. They turned toward the door where Jane
Crichton-Sloane stood, clutching a long white robe around
her.

Her husband rushed to her. "Jane! What are you
doing here?"

"I woke up and thought I heard voices," she said in a
small voice.

"Please, my dear, go back to bed."

She didn't move. "Who is this man, Stanley? What does

ıe want?" She caught sight of Muriel. "What are these peo-
ıle doing here at this time of night?" Her voice was now
.hrill.

"It would take too long to explain," Crichton-Sloane said
gently. "I'll tell you tomorrow. Be a good girl now and go
ıp to bed. I'll be there in a moment."

She shook her head. "No, Stanley, there's something
wrong. I can feel it. Tell me what it is . . ."

Crichton-Sloane wavered for a moment, then made his
decision. "Come, I'll take you back upstairs."

He put his arm around his wife's shoulders and led her
ıut of the room. From the distance, Jeff and Muriel could
ıear her high protesting voice and the deep soothing tones
ıf her husband.

Finally they heard the sound of returning footsteps and
Crichton-Sloane was back, alone. He seemed composed but
there was an ugly glint in his eye. "I should never have
.llowed you to come here tonight."

"But you will hear me out, won't you, Mr. Crichton-
Sloane," Jeff said with assurance. And, not waiting for the
ninister's response, he continued his narrative.

"So there was Egleton in Haiti; the British were happy, the
Russians were happy. Everything's O.K. until one fine day
.omething happens that nobody could have foreseen. An
.ging English anthropologist, doing research in Haiti, takes
.t into his head to go to a cockfight in some out-of-the-way
.orner in Pétionville. And there, in the crowd, he sees an
.ld comrade-in-arms and ex–fellow student of the espionage
.chool in Moscow. Lolik! To be sure, he has changed a lot,
.ut there's something in his face that awakens old memories.
.o Jennings waves to him, tries to run after him, and tells all
.bout it in a letter to his wife.

"Egleton saw him too. He also recognized his old friend,

and that's when he committed his fatal error: he told the
K.G.B. He asked them to do something about Jennings for
fear the man might start talking. But Egleton misjudged the
Russians' mentality. His pals at the K.G.B. started asking
themselves questions: What if Jennings had talked already?
And if he had recognized Egleton so easily after all these
years, wasn't it likely that somebody else might?

"In their minds, there was only one solution. Finito. So a
team of killers was dispatched from Djerdjinski Square with
the urgent mission of liquidating not only Jennings but Egleton as well. The mission was accomplished on the night of
October 14th."

Muriel buried her face in her hands. Jeff rose from his
chair, went over to her and patted her shoulder. "I'm sorry
but that's the way it happened, Muriel." Then, turning to
Crichton-Sloane, he went on: "But nobody was to know that
Jennings had been killed. That's why they weighted his
body before throwing it into the sea. On the other hand
Egleton's body was to be unrecognizable except for his right
hand so that the British would be able to identify him and
draw their own conclusions.

"The Russians' logic was faultless. The murder would be
passed off as a ritual sacrifice in case the Haitians discovered
the body first. And the British were to be informed in such
a way that they'd think the Russians were settling old accounts, that they had found the traitor — the spy who had
exposed the K.G.B.'s secrets during his trial — and then
taken their revenge.

"There are strange coincidences sometimes," Jeff said,
lighting a new panatela. "If the British had received the
Russians' 'message' in the way the Russians intended, I'm
convinced they would have done their best to hush the
whole thing up. Egleton had operated secretly, he would

lie secretly. They couldn't reveal the fact that he had been killed in Haiti since, officially, he was already dead and buried in England. Nor could they admit he was a British agent, because then the Russians would realize that he'd been leading them by the nose all those years.

"But, as luck would have it, the British agent, Father Finchley, wasn't home that night. The wrong people discovered the body, and our labs in Washington were able to identify the fingerprints.

"Less than twenty-four hours later, I was in England where I learned the truth about Egleton — or at least what the English thought was the truth. Then I met you, and you said; 'Help me! Help me find Egleton's murderer.'"

Jeff rose to his feet, walked over to the desk and planted himself in front of Crichton-Sloane.

"Yes, I wanted to help you. Your sincerity impressed me. I wanted to do everything in my power not to disappoint you. Of course, I didn't realize that the moment you closed the door after me, you set a team of K.G.B. killers on my tail! And you were the only one — except for the Security chiefs — who was being kept informed of my whereabouts, day by day and hour by hour. I myself had asked Jim Sullivan to do it. I thought it was the least I could do for you.

"After the ambush in Soledad, when I was coming to at the hospital in Malaga, I realized somebody had betrayed me. I suspected everyone — my colleagues, the British. Everyone but you. It never crossed my mind that you might be the traitor.

"I learned about Lolik from a letter Jennings had written Isabella Guerrero seven days before his disappearance. I spent two whole months trying to find out who he was because I was convinced he was Egleton's and Jennings's murderer. Then yesterday, in that train in Vienna, General

Lavrenti Polianov told me that Lolik's real name was Dennis
Harold Egleton. Lolik and Egleton were one and the same.
Suddenly the whole thing became clear. That's when I re
alized that you, Mr. Crichton-Sloane, were the instigator o
Egleton's murder. You were the reason that Theodoris wa
murdered; you were the reason Sheila MacAlister commit
ted suicide; it was because of you they had to dispose o
David Jennings; because of you Egleton's body was burned
and Burt Partridge was poisoned. And finally, it was be
cause of you that Muriel and I were to die. All those mur
ders, all that blood spilled to save your neck. So that you
sir, would be able to go on serving the K.G.B.

"But as you see, here I am. Not in the best of shape, to be
sure, but alive. And in the end, you've failed. This time
you're really finished, Mr. Crichton-Sloane."

The Secretary sat down at his desk and flicked a switch in
the wall by his side. The room was suddenly bathed in light
"Go and tell that story, Mr. Saunders, and see how many
people will believe you."

Jeff smiled faintly.

"Is that what you really want? You want me to tell my
story? Well, what are we waiting for, Muriel?" He made a
if to leave. For a moment, there was absolute silence. N
one moved: not the girl trembling by the fireplace, no
Saunders standing legs apart in the middle of the room, no
Crichton-Sloane sitting ramrod-straight in his chair. Then
suddenly, the minister spun to the left, opened a drawer and
thrust his hand in it without taking his eyes off Saunders.

"You know," he said, "there comes a time in all thriller
when the villain seizes a gun and aims it at the amateur de
tective . . ."

Jeff broke in, aping his tone: "And in all thrillers, it's a
that very moment that the men from Scotland Yard come

bursting into the room. No, no, Crichton-Sloane, don't do anything so unworthy of you. Besides, it won't do you a damn bit of good. Muriel, tell him what you did today."

For a moment, Muriel had difficulty finding her voice. Then, pride giving her confidence, she spoke up. "We arrived in Dover this morning. I went straight to London to Sir Brian Auchinleck's house. I gave him a letter from Jeff. He read it and said he would do what Jeff asked."

Jeff turned to Crichton-Sloane: "It is now past midnight. That means that Sir Brian and his men have been waiting by your gate for over two hours."

"Why don't they come in and arrest me?"

"That is not what they're here for. I thought it would be an indignity for England to have her Foreign Secretary arrested for high treason. No, Sir Brian and his men came only to protect us. If we're not out of here within a half hour, they'll force their way in. As for your personal predicament, I'm afraid you'll have to solve it some other way."

Crichton-Sloane stood lost in thought. Whatever was going on inside his heart and head, nothing showed on the surface. He was dignified, calm, his eyes expressionless.

"Come, Muriel, they're waiting for us." Jeff stopped at the door and turned to face Crichton-Sloane for a last time. "I don't recommend suicide," he said. "I think an accident would be more appropriate."

Epilogue

"WE INTERRUPT this program to make an important announcement." The television screen had gone blank for a second, then the B.B.C.'s news announcer came on, holding a sheet of paper in his hand. At the same moment, Stanley Crichton-Sloane's face appeared in the upper right-hand corner of the screen. The announcer's habitual composure had deserted him. He read in a grave voice:

"Her Majesty's Government regrets to announce the death of its Foreign Secretary, Mr. Stanley Crichton-Sloane. He was killed early this morning in a motor accident in the Cotswolds. The Minister, who was at the wheel of his car, was making his annual visit to the county Agricultural Fair. Apparently, his Rolls Royce missed a sharp turn and hurtled down a steep incline. The shock of the impact flung his body clear of the car. He was taken to the hospital but was found to be dead on arrival. The cause of the accident has not been determined, but it is thought that the thick fog covering the area and the slippery conditions of the roads caused by the recent heavy rains may have been a factor.

"Funeral services will be held on a day to be announced at Westminster in the presence of members of the Government and a representative of the Royal Family. Her Majesty the Queen has sent a message of condolence to Mrs. Crichton-Sloane. The date has not yet been announced."

The announcer paused. "At eight o'clock tonight, there will be a special program on the life of the late Foreign Secretary . . ."

The Minister's funeral took place in an atmosphere of national mourning. Thousands of men, women and children followed the coffin of the man so recently called "Britain's greatest hope." Eloquent speeches were delivered over his grave which was heaped high with flowers and wreaths. Jeff Saunders and Muriel Jennings attended the ceremony When it was over, Jeff laid a large bunch of flowers on the freshly dug grave. They were, of course, chrysanthemums.

For many s.f. addicts the Golden Age began in 1938 when John Campbell became editor of Astounding Stories. For Isaac Asimov, the formative and most memorable period came in the decade before the Golden Age – the 1930s. It is to the writers of this generation that BEFORE THE GOLDEN AGE is dedicated.

Some – Jack Williamson, Murray Leinster, Stanley Weinbaum and Asimov himself – have remained famous to this day. Others such as Neil Jones, S. P. Meek and Charles Tanner, have been deservedly rescued from oblivion.

BEFORE THE GOLDEN AGE was originally published in the United States in a single mammoth volume of almost 1,200 pages. The British paperback edition will appear in four books, the first of which covers the years 1930 to 1933.

In this third volume, Isaac Asimov has selected a feast of rousing tales such as BORN BY THE SUN by Jack Williamson, with its marvellous vision of the solar system as a giant incubator; Murray Leinster's story of parallel time-tracks SIDEWISE IN TIME; and Raymond Z. Gallin's OLD FAITHFUL which features one of science fiction's most memorable aliens – Number 774.

'Sheer nostalgic delight . . . stories by authors long-forgotten mingle with those by ones who are well-known, and still writing. A goldmine for anyone interested in the evolution of s.f.'
Sunday Times

'Contains some of the very best s.f. from the Thirties . . . emphatically value for money.'
Evening Standard